RISING TIDES

SEA OF MERMAID SECRETS

~ 2 ~

USA TODAY BESTSELLING AUTHOR
ALICIA RADES

Copyright © 2026 Alicia Rades

All rights reserved. No part of this book may be used or reproduced in any matter whatsoever without written permission from the author except in brief quotations used in articles and reviews.

This is a work of fiction. Names, characters, places, and incidents are either the product of the author's imagination or are used fictitiously, and any resemblance to actual persons, living or dead, business establishments, events or locales is entirely coincidental.

Published by Crystallite Publishing LLC.

Cover design by Orina Kafe.

SEA OF MERMAID SECRETS SERIES

Deep Waters
Rising Tides
Crashing Waves

ALSO BY ALICIA RADES

HIDDEN LEGENDS: ACADEMY OF MAGICAL CREATURES

The Fire Prophecy

The Water Legacy

The Earth Legend

The Air Omen

The Elemental War

The Soul Sacrifice

HIDDEN LEGENDS: COLLEGE OF WITCHCRAFT

The Coven's Secret

The Reaper's Shadow

The Cauldron's Curse

The Demon's Spell

The Warlock's Trial

The Witch's Fate

HIDDEN LEGENDS: PRISON FOR SUPERNATURAL OFFENDERS

The Villain Institute

The Criminal Lair

The Infernal Underground

The Assassin's Destiny

The Devil's City

The Elven Gate

VENGEANCE AND VAMPIRES

Ravenite

Resilience

Resolute

Retribute

CRYSTAL FROST

Fire in Frost

Desire in Frost

Inspired by Frost

Fading Frost

DAVINA UNIVERSE

Divine Fate Trilogy:

Chosen by Grace

Touched by Grace

Awakened by Grace

Divine Descendants Duology:

Concealing Magic

Exposing Magic

CHAPTER 1

The soft sound of a beautiful song carried over the ocean water, welcoming a strange sense of peace that didn't feel possible in the wake of all that happened.

Just yesterday, my friends and I had escaped the clutches of the Sea Haven Council, who had intended to strip us of our merfolk magic and use their siren calls to compel us to forget all the corruption we'd uncovered. My father helped us escape, but council head Carson Ray had come after us. He'd intended to kill us so that his secret regarding the theft of our people's magic would never be discovered.

For the first time in my life, I'd summoned the supersonic scream of my mermaid ancestors. I overpowered the man who'd stolen my magic and sent sharks after him to finish him off. I still clutched the aquamarine stone I'd taken from him. The stone had shielded him from the weapon he was using to take merfolk's magic against their knowledge.

In the midst of it all, I lost my dear friend Delphina—the dolphin who had saved my life—and we had no choice but to leave our friends and family behind. Now, it was just Liana, Noah, Tristan, and me on a small sailboat, surrounded by an endless ocean that stretched to the horizon in all directions.

We'd sailed through the night in pursuit of the Luna pod. This tiny sailboat shouldn't be out this far on the open water, but our powers helped calm the waves, and Tristan's guidance kept us heading in the right direction. I had no idea how much longer the journey might take.

It all should've sent me breaking down, and it did, in a way. I mourned the loss of Delphina, and I missed my parents and my friend Christina. But at the same time, the sound of the song reminded me that I wasn't alone in the aftermath. Whatever came next, my friends and I would face it together.

Liana sat at the front of the sailboat, dangling her feet over the edge as her arms curled around the metal railing. Her soothing voice calmed the ache in my gut.

Gifted powers of the sea
Our people ruled the waters
The landmen came with their massive ships
And had our people slaughtered

Soon we'll witness turning tides
When the land and sea conspire
Once again in harmony
Like the Gods once so desired

Tristan stood at the steering wheel. Sunlight glinted off his muscled torso, and his long blond hair danced in the gentle breeze. "What's that you're singing?"

"It's an old sea shanty," Liana answered. "You know it?"

"It sounds familiar," Tristan mused. "How does it go...? *We descended into the sea depths.*"

"Ocean depths," I corrected. I'd been leaning against the railing, inhaling the scent of saltwater as I listened to Liana's melody. "How do you know that song? I thought it was something only Sea Haven's people knew. It's about our history."

"We share a history, Bree," Tristan reminded me. "Up until the Luna pod and the Sea Haven pod split, we were one people."

"I hadn't realized the song was that old," I responded.

I knew the history. Merfolk had been hunted to near-extinction by human sailors. Pods from around the globe united, finding strength in numbers, until there was only one pod left. Over two-hundred years ago, disagreements broke out over a child born of a human father and mermaid mother. Half the pod took to land to blend in with the humans, and the other half remained at sea. I'd always believed the merfolk at sea had died off, until Tristan arrived and proved otherwise.

Noah, Liana, and I were descendants of the land pod. I'd been led to believe my whole life that our magic had been diluted through the generations until all we had left was the ability to breathe underwater for short amounts of time, communicate with sea life, and control small amounts of water. I was told the mertail, siren song, and supersonic scream of our ancestors had been lost as time went on, only to discover it was all a lie.

In reality, the council has been using a weapon all these years to harness our magic and convert it to energy for profit. We'd defeated the man at the head of the operation, but we still had an entire council to face and a weapon to destroy, and we didn't know where to find it. We couldn't return to Sea Haven without the council capturing or killing us the moment our feet hit land. We needed help.

But we weren't the only ones who needed assistance. Tristan had come to Sea Haven in search of help with his own pod, because an underwater mining operation nearby was polluting their waters. His people thought Sea Haven could help them, but after everything that happened once the council captured Tristan, the four of us had no choice but to flee.

Tristan suggested we return with him to his pod and gather support to defeat the council and restore our people's magic. Then we could help negotiate with the mining company and revive the Luna pod's ecosystem, without exposing their existence.

Noah popped his head up from under the deck, a gorgeous smirk on his face. The sailboat wasn't very large, but it was big enough to have a bed and a tiny bathroom in the cabin. "You aren't going to believe what I found." He held up a collection of cheese and crackers, along with fresh water for everyone.

Liana scrambled to her feet. "Noah! You're a life saver. I'm starving."

"There's more down here," Noah said. "I found a stash of beef jerky and bags of dried fruit."

Tristan stepped away from the wheel. "We should eat before we get to my pod."

The four of us gathered around a bench at the back of the boat and filled our bellies. Tristan sat on one side of me, and Noah on the other. I felt my cheeks heat as I sank deeper into the seat between them. I remembered the warmth of Tristan's hand in mine as we ran for our lives to escape City Hall. At the same time, I thought of the way my heart fluttered when Noah inspected the cut on my palm at Liana's grandparents' house, before Carson captured us.

I shouldn't be thinking of either of them in that way right now. I nibbled on crackers to distract myself. Soon, I found myself humming the tune to the old sea shanty Liana had been singing.

"I haven't heard that song in ages," Noah remarked. "My mom used to sing it to me when I was little. I can't remember the second verse, though."

"We descended into ocean depths," I started, and Liana quickly joined in. Soon, the four of us were singing the second verse and chorus in harmony.

> *We descended into ocean depths*
> *Our home submerged so deep*
> *Lured sailors to their deaths*
> *Anchored our souls to the sea*
>
> *Soon we'll witness turning tides*
> *When the land and sea conspire*
> *Once again in harmony*
> *Like the Gods once so desired*

"Isn't there a third verse?" Noah wondered.

"I don't remember it," I admitted.

Liana waved her hand nonchalantly. "We know enough of it."

She broke out into song again, this time louder than before. We all joined in, starting back at the beginning. It wasn't particularly a happy song, but the upbeat tune made it feel lighter than the words portrayed, and the chorus brought a sense of hope with it. Liana took my hand, and I jumped up to spin around the deck with her. It felt good to come together in song, like the music had a healing quality to it.

Abruptly, the tone aboard the deck shifted. Tristan stiffened, falling dead silent. His blue-green eyes locked on the horizon.

We all turned to look. It was difficult to spot at first, but far in the distance I noticed a disturbance against the surface of the sea. At first, I thought it was a large wave, then wondered if it could be a ship. Liana and Noah wandered to the front of the boat to peer closer.

Tristan took the wheel in his hands. "We're almost home. Hold on tight."

The ocean rose up at his command, and we were caught in a powerful wave as Tristan's magic rocketed us forward. My hands curled around the metal railing to hold myself steady, and the wind rushed through my hair.

As we came closer to the object in the distance, I realized it wasn't a wave or a ship at all. It was an *island*. Jagged rocks rose out of the ocean, and the island was covered in greenery and sand. It wasn't very large—I guessed a mile long, at most—but the island was beautiful against the backdrop of the blue sea.

I turned toward Tristan and shouted over the wind. "Your people have been this close to us all this time?"

"We've lived here for centuries, before the pod split in two," Tristan replied. "When your people left the ocean for land, they didn't go far, though it's not as close as you might think. We're hundreds of miles off the mainland now. Our magic increased the speed of the current to get us here much faster than we would by other means."

Liana pushed blond strands of hair from her face. "It's beautiful. I didn't expect the Luna pod to reside on an island."

"The island is a landmark," Tristan said. "Our city is underwater, but there's a reef around the island that supplies most of our food."

Noah turned to Tristan. "With a landmark like this so close to your city, don't you run the risk of someone discovering your pod?"

"Your council's weapon that suppressed your powers has prevented your people from using your siren call, but the Luna pod still has the power of compulsion," Tristan said. "We enchanted this island long ago with an ancestral song that deters anyone without merfolk blood, and we ensure our secrecy by reinforcing the magic every year on the autumn equinox. The enchantment even conceals us from modern technology, so radar and satellite images can't spot us. To the rest of the world, our little pocket of ocean doesn't exist. If you listen closely, you can hear the song."

Tristan waved his hand through the air, and the current propelling us forward slowed. The bow of the boat sliced through the water as we approached the island. Far off in the distance—past the sound of lapping ocean waves and the caw of seagulls—I heard a distant melody.

The siren song was everywhere and nowhere all at once, reaching my ears through the sea, wind, and sky at the same time. Voices overlaid one another in a harmonious chorus that seemed to permeate deep into my bones. I looked around for the source of the voices, half expecting to find a choir of mermaids singing from the beach, but the song seemed to come straight from nature itself. I understood then what Tristan meant by *enchanted*. The island itself sang the song of the seafolk.

The song had no words, but it didn't need them. I could feel the potent energy, a prayer of *protection*, permeating through every note.

I'd never heard anything more beautiful. I felt something warm ignite within my chest, like there was a part of me missing all my life until I heard the song. Tristan had said the Luna pod existed here before it split in two—before half the pod took to land and settled in Sea Haven. Which meant this song belonged to *my* ancestors.

I had merfolk blood in me, and I'd restored my core—the source of my magic that had been taken from me—which meant I couldn't be compelled away from this island like others could. The siren song moved me in ways I never thought possible.

A tear fell down my cheek. My whole life, I believed that the siren call of our ancestors was gone. But all this time, Carson Ray had been stealing it from us—stealing *this*. He'd told me once that the people of Sea Haven didn't know what they were missing, as if that fact could justify his actions. Experiencing the incredible beauty of this magic now made me hate him even more, because now that I *knew* what he was taking from us, I could see he was even more deeply vile than I ever realized before.

Tristan reached out to wipe my tears. My breath shuddered beneath his touch as he brought me back to the present.

"Sorry," he said quickly. "I didn't mean to make you sad."

"You didn't. It's this song... it's so, *so* beautiful." I looked up into those blue-green eyes.

Tristan's soft gaze locked on mine. I could swear the song grew louder, reverberating through my heart space.

"It's gorgeous!" Liana exclaimed.

I turned to the front of the boat to see that Liana and Noah had moved past the beauty of the song and were marveling at a beautiful lagoon straight in front of us. They hadn't seen Tristan wipe my tears away.

Tristan cleared his throat. "We'll drop anchor in the lagoon."

We drifted into the lagoon, and the four of us worked together to drop the sails and anchor the boat close to shore. I peered at the crystal-clear blue-green water below us, where schools of colorful fish darted from one side of the boat to the other. I'd never seen anything quite so beautiful.

I didn't realize my fingers had tightened around the railing until Tristan came up beside me. He must've noticed. "He can't hurt you here, Bree," he stated lightly. "That councilman of yours is long gone, and his weapon is far behind us. This is Luna pod territory, and here, you're one of us. Do you want to see what you can do now that you're free?"

My heart gave a jolt in my chest. "I do."

Tristan smirked. "Then follow me."

He jumped into the lagoon, and I laughed as a big splash sprayed water droplets all over my legs. Tristan tossed his long hair back as he resurfaced. Within an instant, his pants had vanished, and his legs were replaced by a long tail covered in green scales. The scales glinted against the sunlight, shimmering a slight blue that matched his eyes.

Tristan floated on his back and smacked his long fins against the surface of the water. "Come on in! The water's great."

Liana stepped up first. "Here goes nothing!"

She jumped into the water, and my breath caught as I witnessed her legs transform in an instant. In their place appeared a golden tail with scales that shimmered a metallic bronze. While Tristan's tail split in two directions on the end, Liana had a singular large fin that widened at the edges. Her t-shirt had disappeared, and in its place were golden scales that crept up her torso. The scales left most of her belly exposed but created a modest mosaic across her chest.

Her head broke the surface of the water, and she gasped in amazement as she stared down at her scales. "Oh, my god! I can't believe I have a real tail!"

"Liana, it's so beautiful!" I called from the boat.

Her eyes widened in amazement, and then she ducked beneath the surface again to test her fins out. She swam faster than I thought possible, racing from the boat to the other end of the lagoon in seconds. She circled back around, then jumped out of the water, before diving back in with a glorious splash a few yards in front of us.

Her gleeful laughter filled the air as she ran her fingers over her scales. "It's perfect! Come on, you guys. Let's see what yours look like!"

I didn't know why, but I hesitated. It didn't make any sense, because seeing Liana's tail should've sent me rushing into the water in a second. All I'd ever known was the ocean, and having full access to my merfolk powers would only bring me closer to the sea. It's all I ever wanted.

Noah noticed my unease, and he graciously held out a hand toward me. "Together?" he offered.

Taking his hand was nearly as frightening as jumping into the water, but I found myself slipping my hand into his warm palm. His touch was comforting and reminded me of home.

"Together," I agreed.

Noah and I stepped over the railing, and we took the leap.

I screamed in exhilaration for the brief moment we were falling through the air. Cool water hit me from all angles, but my scream continued growing even louder as I became submerged. I'd only used my sonic scream once, and I hadn't really known how powerful it could be. Here underwater, my voice was as clear as it was on the surface.

Noah's laughter filled my ears, and I realized he was using *his* supersonic scream. His hand slipped out of mine, and I looked over to see a majestic cobalt tail swimming past me. I watched in awe as his tail swayed in the water, the ends of his fins splitting off in six directions.

Noah spun around, his gorgeous tail spanning behind him. When his eyes locked on mine, his features fell. I glanced at Tristan and Liana, who were both peering through the water in bewilderment.

"What?" I asked innocently.

Then I looked downward to discover that my legs were still treading water.

I had failed to summon my tail.

CHAPTER 2

"I don't understand," I said. "You all made it look so easy."

Liana swam over to me, her fin trailing like a sheet of gold behind her. "It was intuitive for me, but maybe it isn't for everyone. There must be different techniques we can try."

I turned to Noah. His form was nearly breathtaking as I took in his bare muscled chest and deep blue scales. "How did it feel for you?"

"I just had to think about it, and my fins appeared," he admitted. "There must be a trick to it."

Tristan shook his head. "There are no tricks here. Our magic is not deceptive."

"Then the water must activate your tails, and I—I don't have one," I stammered.

Fear gripped my throat at the thought that I may not be as magical as I believed. I wondered if Carson had been right and it was better if we didn't know what we were missing. I'd only just discovered I may be able to access the height of my ancestral power, and now it felt like it was being taken from me all over again, even if it was never mine to begin with.

"The water does not activate our powers," Tristan said. "*We* do."

To demonstrate, his tail shrank and became legs again, covered by his jeans. The four of us were submerged in the ocean completely, so our ability to shift from human legs to fish tails clearly had nothing to do with the land and sea.

"To shift is a conscious choice," Tristan explained. "All you have to do is ask your tail to appear, and it will."

The instructions sounded so simple, so I didn't understand why it seemed impossible. I closed my eyes and visualized my legs melding into one and imagined scales sprouting down my lower half. I expected to feel some indication of magic tingling down my body, but I felt nothing. When I opened my eyes, my legs were still treading water, and my baggy wet t-shirt clung to my shoulders.

"The stories must be right," I said. "Sea Haven's people lost their abilities through the generations."

"If that were true, then Noah and I wouldn't be able to summon our tails," Liana pointed out.

"My family line must be more diluted than yours," I theorized.

Tristan furrowed his brow. "We know Carson and his family have been lying to your people for generations. He admitted it himself. If the stories you learned as a kid were true, then you wouldn't be able to use your sonic scream, and I saw you blast back Carson with your voice before you sent the sharks after him. Plus, you're projecting your words through the water now, which means you can access your merfolk scream. You should be able to summon other powers, too. We're hundreds of miles from Sea Haven, so the weapon your council used to suppress your powers all these years shouldn't affect you now."

"Carson called the weapon a *sea stone*," I said. "Maybe that stone left lasting effects on me."

Tristan ran his fingers over his chin and through his beard. "I'm not sure, but perhaps my people will have an answer. We should visit the king right away."

I knew that our ancestors once operated under a monarchy, so it shouldn't surprise me to learn they still had royalty today, but it still took me off guard when Tristan mentioned a king. I realized I wasn't sure what to expect from the Luna pod at all.

Noah hesitated. "Is it safe to visit your pod? We don't know the full extent of Bree's access to magic. You said your people live deep underwater. The depths could be too much for her—too much for all of us, if Liana and I are affected long-term by the sea stone as well."

"I want to go," I countered. "I've been in deep waters before. As long as I come up to breathe every couple of hours, it should be safe."

"That's right," Tristan remarked. "Where you come from, you can't breathe underwater indefinitely. I'll take you to meet our king, but we'll go slow and stay close to the surface until we get to Luna City. If you ever feel like it's too much, we'll turn back to the surface."

"All right," I agreed. "Take us to Luna City."

Tristan's legs transformed back into a tail. "Your legs won't be able to keep up, so you can hang on to me."

I tugged on my t-shirt. "This is going to slow us down."

I stripped off my baggy t-shirt and already felt lighter in the water. I was left in a pair of shorts and a modest sports bra. Then I kicked to the surface and tossed the t-shirt onto the boat.

"Ready?" Tristan asked when I ducked my head back underwater.

This was the place of my ancestors. I didn't know if I'd ever be ready.

I nodded anyway. "Let's go."

Tristan turned his back to me, and I gingerly wrapped my arms around his shoulders. His body was warm against mine. He flicked his tail, and we sped toward open waters, reaching the edge of the lagoon in seconds. I almost lost my grip as my legs flew out behind me. Noah and Liana followed.

Tristan slowed for a second and gently grabbed my hand to pull me closer. "Hang on, Bree."

I didn't know if it was an effect of his siren call, but I could swear when he said my name it sounded like a song. Strange, because siren magic shouldn't work on me, even if my magic wasn't at its full power. Carson had compelled me once, but he was only able to do it after he'd stolen my core and the source of my magic, which I'd gotten back.

"Is this all right?" I asked as I wrapped my legs around his hips, then curled my arms tightly around his shoulders. I wasn't used to being this close to anyone, but I was going to have to get comfortable with it real fast, or I'd slow us down.

Tristan glanced over his shoulder, his blue-green gaze locking on mine. "That's perfect."

Beside us, Noah frowned, but Liana winked at me playfully. Before I could even begin to process either of their reactions, Tristan had taken off again. We sped forward and out of the lagoon, bubbles tickling my skin from all angles. The ocean floor dropped off, and the water grew dark beneath us, but Tristan stayed close to the surface where sunlight still danced across our bodies. Noah swam on one side of us, and Liana on the other. The two of them had no problem keeping up, even though it felt like we were swimming fast enough to cover miles of ocean in mere minutes.

I'd ridden on the backs of dolphins more times than I could count, but being carried through the water by a merman was a completely different experience. He swam faster and turned sharper, and he cut through the water in a way that felt like he and the ocean were one. I envied his grace and agility as much as I deeply admired it.

Through the darkness of the ocean depths, I caught sight of a tall, rocky structure in the distance. As we came closer, the waters cleared, and I gasped when I realized the towering structure was the spire of a building set in the heart of an underwater city.

Since I was a child, I wondered what the cities of our ancestors would've looked like, but my imagination could never live up to the real thing. Below us, the sunlight shone through crystal-clear waters and glimmered off every surface, making it appear as if the city itself was sparkling.

Luna City was expertly crafted out of natural rock, with ornate windows carved into cliffsides and beautiful columns sculpted around cave entrances. Colorful coral clung to the rocks, and seaweed swayed with the gentle current. Fish in all colors of the rainbow darted through rock crevices or swam in schools that glided through the water as if the sea life was engaged in a beautiful dance. White sand stretched across the ocean floor and reflected the blue brilliance of the ocean waves above us.

But there was one thing that caught my attention above all else, something far more beautiful than the natural structures, impeccable architecture, or colorful marine life, and that was the people. Merfolk with all different sizes and colors of fins swam from one opening in the rock to another, or traveled across the city in groups, making their swim patterns appear like natural roadways. They moved in sync like schools of fish, as if their intuition alone told them where the roads led.

My gaze darted from one beautiful person to the next, taking in their gorgeous scales and how the colors complimented each person's unique features impeccably. Like back in Sea Haven, the Luna pod was home to merfolk with ancestry from all over the world. Several people with blond hair shared similar pink tails in varying shades, though each person's fin pattern was unique. Stunning women with black braids had magnificent copper tails that shimmered blue or green, while others had mesmerizing bright green tails or incredible purple scales that left me entranced. A man with dark hair swam beneath us, and I marveled at his orange and white tail with long, flowing fins similar to that of a koi fish.

All throughout the city, people were going about their day as usual. I spotted a merman carrying a net and trading fish with other merfolk. Nearby, young children played with a dolphin. They slid down the dolphin's tail on their bellies, then laughed gleefully as the dolphin flicked her tail upward, sending the children spinning through the water. A choir had joined together in an open area near the ocean floor, and they sang in perfect harmony while others spun their tails and kicked up sand in joyful celebration.

"This city is incredible!" Liana exclaimed.

Noah's eyes sparkled with intrigue as he peered down upon the city below. "It's really something."

The three of us were at a complete loss of words, mesmerized by the colors, the architecture, the people...

the *water*. Being here filled my heart to the point I thought it might burst, because it was all my heart desperately longed for, even if I didn't realize I craved it before now. It was everything Sea Haven could be if we restored our people's magic.

"We're almost there," Tristan said.

We rounded a large rock structure that rose off the ocean floor as tall as a skyscraper. As we turned the corner, a magnificent formation came into view, one that had towering spires and elegant doorways carved all throughout its surface. It was more stunning than anything I'd ever seen back home, and I realized it had to be the royal palace.

My breath caught. "Tristan, it's incredible."

He peered back at me with a smile. "Welcome home."

CHAPTER 3

Tristan led us forward, and we approached a large archway at the front of the palace. There were no doors, but two muscular mermen guarded the entrance. They must've recognized Tristan, because they nodded kindly to him and let us through. The two men gave me a strange look, and I realized how unusual it must be to see someone with legs this deep underwater. The guards didn't ask for an explanation, though, and Tristan continued forward.

A long cavern stretched in front of us, carved from the rock. It looked a lot like a hallway, though the floor wasn't flat, but rather rounded in a way that mirrored the arched ceiling. It occurred to me that merfolk spent all their time suspended in the water and didn't need flat surfaces to walk on, so their architecture differed from anything I'd seen back home. Ornate frames outlined doorways that led to other places in the castle. Small holes only large enough for tiny fish to fit through had been carved out in the ceiling to let the sunlight shine through.

As we swam deeper into the heart of the palace, the holes in the rock became less frequent. Instead, bioluminescent algae clung to the stone walls to illuminate our path. A mesmerizing teal hue filled the corridor, pulsing ever so slightly as slow water currents passed over the algae.

I was so entranced by the glowing algae that it took me a moment to realize Tristan had slowed. At the end of the corridor stood a large opening in the rock, nearly as big as the archway we'd entered the palace through. Voices drifted out into the hall.

"This is taking too long, King Aalto!" a woman demanded. "Tristan and the others should've been back by now."

A man with a deep voice responded. "The journey is a long one. We must give them time, Cordelia."

"If Tristan and the others aren't back within the week, I'll organize a search party myself," a younger male voice offered.

"You have a job to do, Zale," the king countered. "I'll send others if they aren't back soon."

"There's no need. I'm back," Tristan announced as he swam into the chamber.

The four of us stopped in the center of the room, and I unwound myself from Tristan's back. Floating in the water seemed to come to the others as easily as standing on solid ground, but I found myself treading water to stay in one place as I observed the chamber.

A tall window stretched the entirety of one wall. Sun rays cut through the sea and shimmered around the cavern. In front of the window stood a large scallop shell larger than any I'd ever seen. It was positioned like a throne, which a powerful-looking man with a graying beard and silver fins sat upon. He wore a matching silver crown atop his head.

Beside him was the woman who'd spoken—Cordelia, he'd called her. She looked around my age, with golden hair that spilled over her shoulders and a pale purple tail. She must've been a princess or some sort of noble, because she wore a tiara embedded with shiny shells and crystals atop her head.

The younger man, Zale, looked similar to Tristan, though his beard was a darker shade, and he had an orange tail with red-tipped fins. A dozen other merfolk who must've been members of the king's council surrounded the room. They were perched upon a ledge that circled the perimeter of the chamber, observing the meeting.

"Tristan!" Cordelia flicked her tail and crossed the chamber in a second. Her features fell as she reached up to place her hands on either side of his face to look over his injuries. Tristan still had a black eye courtesy of the Sea Haven Council, and the bullet wound on his shoulder was visible for all to see. "You've been hurt!"

Cordelia's gaze flickered to me behind him, and she eyed me up and down with a scowl. "You brought... guests."

Tristan gave a diplomatic nod. "There's much to discuss."

Zale swam forward with an arm outstretched. "It's good to have you back."

Tristan and Zale gripped each other's wrists in a sort of handshake that was unlike ours from back home.

The king straightened on his throne. "Where are the others?"

He had to be talking about the men who'd made the journey to Sea Haven with Tristan, the ones who'd perished in the terrible storm. Tristan had been the only one wearing an aquamarine stone, and it was the one thing that could counteract the council's weapon, though no one had known that at the time.

Tristan dropped his head. "I'm afraid my companions did not make it."

Gasps traveled around the throne room. I could feel the despair settle in the water in the following moment of silence.

Tristan's voice cut through the quiet to explain what had happened. He told them how his companions had failed to summon their powers the closer they came to Sea

Haven and how the council had captured and tortured him.

King Aalto listened curiously, then gestured the four of us forward. "After all that, you've brought surface folk to help us?"

"I wish it were that simple," Tristan said. "They too have been wronged by their council, and we fled."

King Aalto's gaze traveled toward my legs. "Did your council damage your tail? If so, we may be able to help."

The king had an intense, commanding presence, but he was also very kind.

I shook my head. "I'm unable to summon my tail, though we're not sure why. We hoped you might have insight."

The king appeared curious. "I haven't witnessed anyone unable to summon their tail before... yet you can breathe underwater."

"Things are far different in Sea Haven than we predicted," Tristan explained. "Their council has found a way to siphon their magic, and they've spent generations without full access to their power. We don't know the lasting effects this has on their people."

"Hmph," the king huffed thoughtfully. "What is your name?"

I bowed my head. "Bree Waters, Your Majesty. These are my friends Liana Reed and Noah Starr."

The king waved his hand. "It matters not whether you can summon your tail, as long as you can help us."

I furrowed my brow. "Forgive me, but I'm not sure how

we can help. We came to seek *your* assistance. We need the Luna pod's help to find and destroy the Sea Haven Council's weapon, called a sea stone, in order to bring the full height of our merfolk magic back to Sea Haven."

King Aalto leaned back on his throne. "While I'm sympathetic to your predicament, I'm afraid we cannot lend extra men until the threat upon Luna City is resolved. We have already lost good men to your council. I am not prepared to sacrifice others while we ourselves are struggling."

"Tristan mentioned a mining operation," Liana remarked.

"Yes." The king nodded. "An American company called Ocean Rock has begun an underwater mining operation just outside the borders of our enchantment. It's close enough that it's polluting our waters and damaging our ecosystem. Our fish are dying, and soon, our people will begin to starve. However, if you are able to help us, then perhaps we can provide assistance in return."

"I don't know how much time we can afford," I admitted. The council had already proven they wouldn't hesitate to hurt our families because of what we knew, but we couldn't face them alone, either. We'd be killed the second we showed our faces back home, unless we came with an army big enough to take on the council, and strong enough to combat any power they could muster with their weapon. "We've gone our whole lives without proper access to our magic. What can we provide that your pod doesn't already possess?"

"Knowledge of the surface," King Aalto stated simply. "We have tried to drive these humans away with siren compulsion, but they just come back. If we're to save our ecosystem before it's damaged for good, we need to get rid of them forever."

"You're not suggesting... killing them?" Liana asked carefully.

King Aalto pursed his lips. "Killing individual men will not solve this problem. We're up against a corporation, and if we kill these men, more will come. It is the merfolk way to use our compulsion magic as our greatest weapon, but these are not wandering sailors. They know exactly where to find the resources they want, and they will keep coming back unless we can remove these people from our waters permanently. If siren compulsion won't work, we'll have to handle this diplomatically."

The king rose from his throne and wandered over to a mosaic portrait hanging on the wall. It'd been expertly crafted using tiny shells in all different colors to form the face of a woman with a golden crown atop her head. She had a regal look about her, and I assumed this must be a depiction of the queen. King Aalto ran his fingers over the portrait, staring longingly at the image.

"We've lost so much already," he muttered sadly, before turning back to us. "That's why we came to your people, hoping you could teach us the customs of the surface and give us means in which to negotiate with these people. We've always known your pod was still out there, though we haven't contacted your people for over two-hundred years. We've allowed you to believe we perished long ago so that the war between our pods would end. Therefore, you must understand that we would not have come seeking assistance if we had any other option."

"Could you expand your enchantment around the island?" I wondered.

Zale was the one to answer. "The enchantment is a complex spell that can only be anchored to something significant to the pod, such as our island, but the range of that magic has a limit. We can't expand or move the enchantment to get rid of these people, because there's nothing out there by the drillship to anchor our enchantment to."

"Unless you're familiar with other enchanting techniques," King Aalto added.

I shook my head. "We only just learned that the power to access our tails is still in our blood. We know nothing about enchanting."

King Aalto's gaze dropped to my legs again. "It seems there is much you have to learn about your magic. We can teach you, if you'd like."

"That's a waste of time," Cordelia protested. "We need to get moving on getting rid of Ocean Rock for good, not giving people swimming lessons."

"Just because she does not know our ways does not mean she isn't knowledgeable herself," Zale argued.

King Aalto nodded in agreement. "There is much we can learn from people who are different from us, Cordelia."

"Perhaps the princess is right," I said. "Training in our magic can wait until the immediate threats are eliminated. Your people need to focus on driving Ocean Rock away, while we need to find a way back into Sea Haven. We don't know what the council plans to do to our people now that we've discovered their deception, and we can't wait around to find out. If they're willing to take our magic, what else will they take from us? My father is still back there, and he helped us escape. If the council has captured him, then they could be holding him prisoner the way they did with Tristan. They will go after our friends and family for questioning, which puts everyone we love at risk."

"You yourself are at risk without your powers," King Aalto pointed out. "The way I see it, you have a better chance of facing your council if your magic is operating at its full capacity."

"We don't know how long that could take," I pressed. "We need to be moving right away."

"We must wait for the right opportunity," King Aalto insisted. "We can't go in full force without proper preparations. We've tried it before, and it resulted in catastrophe. We will help you, but our armies must be ready for the task, and until Ocean Rock is defeated, we don't have the people to spare. We're doing all we can, and if you want our help, you must play your part as well."

I gritted my teeth. "Forgive me if I'd rather be looking for a way to destroy this weapon than sitting around waiting."

Several gasps traveled around the room. Nobody had

ever accused me of making a good first impression, that was for certain.

"Bree, you can't speak to the king like that," Tristan warned.

Noah flicked his tail, swimming to my side in a second. "She didn't mean it like that. We've been through a lot, and we just want what's best for everyone. I think we can all agree with Bree that we don't want to see more people get hurt."

Noah placed a gentle hand on my upper back to show me he was firmly on my side. His touch did something to me, sending a calming sensation down my spine that felt like a promise that everything would be all right.

I drew a deep breath. "Noah's right. I just don't want to see anyone else get hurt, and that includes your pod. Our people need help, but we won't abandon a desperate nation, either. If there's any way we can help, we will."

"We don't know where their allegiance lies!" Cordelia cut in. "If Bree can't summon a tail, she has more in common with the surface dwellers than with us."

"You know *nothing* about me," I snapped. Noah touched my back again, warning me to reel it in before I ruined our chance at securing an alliance.

Tristan quickly came to my defense. "Bree helped me escape. She and her friends are not a threat to us. We need these people from the surface to teach us more about their ways. In return, I'll train Bree to summon her tail myself if I have to."

Cordelia gaped at him, but King Aalto spoke before she could.

"Very well," the king said. "Tristan, you will be responsible for Bree while she is with us. We will find suitable mentors for Noah and Liana as well. These three will learn from us, and we will learn from them. Then, when the time is right, we will use what we've learned from one another to defeat Ocean Rock *and* your city council."

Tristan nodded. "Yes, Father."

I was caught off guard briefly. King Aalto was Tristan's father? Which made Tristan... a prince?

I barely had a second to think about it before King Aalto was speaking again. "In the meantime, we shall sound the shell and gather the pod to hold a memorial for those we lost. We will meet at the trench at sundown."

CHAPTER 4

The Luna pod handled grief differently than back home. In Sea Haven, a funeral could take several days to plan. Here in Luna City, people gathered quickly following the loss of a loved one. By that evening, news of Tristan's fallen comrades had spread, and thousands of people were traveling to the outskirts of the city to pay their respects.

"I'm sorry about my outburst," I'd told him as we left the throne room. "My mouth tends to get me in a lot of trouble."

"It's okay," Tristan assured me. "My father is sympathetic to your circumstances, and if the others can't empathize with what you've been through, their opinions are irrelevant."

That was encouraging, at least.

After Tristan's wounds had been bandaged by a healer, using seaweed and aquatic healing herbs, we left the palace and he led me toward the memorial site. We were alone, since Noah and Liana had been sent with palace staff to get settled into guest rooms there a few hours ago. They were planning to meet us at the memorial, but since Tristan had been assigned as my mentor, he was responsible for showing me around.

"In Sea Haven, we usually have a grieving period that lasts a few days, sometimes several weeks, before we hold a funeral," I remarked to Tristan as we swam.

Tristan furrowed his brow, like the concept was silly. "We believe no one should be alone to grieve, so we gather as soon as we are able to provide each other support."

We moved along slowly, though he was still faster than me. I used my powers to help control the sea water to push me forward.

Something else occurred to me. "On the surface, we need time to prepare the body for burial. Do merfolk bury their dead?"

Tristan adjusted a sack on his shoulder that had been woven from seaweed. I wasn't sure what was in it, but he'd gone to his quarters in the palace and came back with it shortly before we left. "No, we don't bury our dead. We lay them to rest in the Ancestral Trench. My brothers' bodies were lost in the storm, so we will lay tokens in their place in memory of them."

"Brothers?" I questioned. "Were they princes as well?"

"No, Zale is my only brother by blood. He didn't come to Sea Haven with us because he has another job to do. I'm grateful he stayed behind. He's two years younger than me, but at eighteen, he's old enough to be considered for such a mission."

That made Tristan twenty years old. I thought he looked around my age, but I'd never asked.

"But he's smaller, too," Tristan added. "Even if he'd worn aquamarine to combat the effects of the sea stone, I'm not sure he'd have escaped the storm's current. He was fortunate to stay behind, as to not meet the fate the others did. The men I traveled with were close friends, but brothers all the same."

Tristan sounded sad, but there was a fondness in his tone, too, like he had a lot of happy memories with them.

"I'm sorry for your loss," I said.

"Thank you," Tristan replied. "I appreciate your kindness."

His words caught me off guard, and I stumbled on my following stroke.

Tristan turned to me. "Did I say something wrong?"

"Not at all. I'm just not used to anyone expressing their appreciation so directly. Back home, appreciation is shown subtly, such as through gifts—never explicitly stated."

To show such vulnerability meant you were having some sort of breakdown, like when the council stole my magic and exiled me. Witnessing my father cry that day was a rare sight.

Tristan had gone through a lot and lost his closest friends, but the way he spoke didn't suggest a mental break. It came more naturally to him, like this phrase was common among his people. It shook me a bit to realize how uncommon that was in my pod.

"I just realized now how normal it is in my family to lock their feelings away until it becomes too much to bear. It never occurred to me that things don't have to be that way." I tried it out on my tongue. "I... appreciate you showing me a new way."

Tristan offered a kind smile. "Of course. We are here to help each other, Bree. That is what merfolk do. Come."

He extended a hand toward me, and I took it. He swished his tail, and we cut through the water faster than I could swim.

Tristan stopped near a rocky structure scattered with seashells. "In the Luna pod, we share in our grief and believe that together we can transmute our heartache into something beautiful, because it is times like this when we must come together. I am not the only one who lost someone. You too lost your dolphin friend, and I think it's only right that we include her in the memorial."

I went speechless as I stared down at the shimmering shells—the same kind Delphina used to bring me as gifts. Slowly, I swam forward and ran my fingers over the shells.

"I grew up believing sadness was something to be pushed down, felt only behind closed doors," I admitted. "I remember when my grandma passed when I was fifteen, and I spent three days locked in my room sobbing. I left my room to get something to eat and found my father crying at the kitchen sink. When he realized I was there, he wiped his eyes and drew me into a hug. That hug helped more than any crying ever could, but we both dashed our tears away and never spoke of it again."

I choked back a sob. "Delphina, the smart creature that she was, had caught on that I was mourning. She brought me seashells every day and left them on a rock just offshore near my house. We'd amassed quite a collection that week, and I always cherished the kindness she showed me."

I reached for a twisted seashell with a pearl-like shimmer and clutched it close to my chest. Delphina would've loved it.

Tristan placed a gentle hand on my shoulder. "It's okay, Bree. Here in the Luna pod, you don't have to hold it back."

Tears welled in my eyes. I didn't cry easily, and when I did I usually choked it down so it wouldn't show. It was difficult to refrain from instinctually dashing the tears away, but I knew that Tristan would understand. As my tears flowed and mixed with the surrounding salt water, I felt a weight ease off my chest. It wasn't completely gone— I didn't know if it'd ever be—but it helped.

I blinked the remaining tears from my eyes. "Thank you. This is exactly what I needed."

Tristan guided me onward, until we reached a long stretch of sand, where thousands of merfolk had already gathered. The sun was starting to set, but my eyes adjusted to the darkness. Ahead, the sea seemed to go on endlessly.

Tristan led us to the front of the crowd, where there was a space reserved for family and friends closest to the deceased. As we came closer to the never-ending darkness, I realized it wasn't just the expanse of the empty sea in front of us. It was a trench that plummeted miles below, so deep that even the sunlight couldn't reach the bottom. Tristan had called it the Ancestral Trench.

He went over to speak to someone I didn't know, while I found Noah and Liana, who were there with their new mentors. Noah's mentor was a muscular guy, but despite his large stature, he had a boyish look about him. He couldn't be any older than Tristan. He had locs in his hair and eyes that matched his emerald-green tail. I'd seen him in the throne room earlier, so I figured he must be among the king's guard. The man extended his hand and introduced himself as Lamar.

Liana's mentor, Maren, was a tall woman with a tail long enough to rival Lamar's. If she transformed her tail into legs, I estimated she'd be at least six feet tall on land. Her body was covered in silver scales that looked like armor. She looked at least a decade older than the rest of us, but she too must've been a member of the king's guard.

Cordelia was here with Zale, and the two of them remained at Tristan's side opposite me when the ceremony began.

An elderly woman positioned herself above the trench, floating high above us all so everyone could see her. Silver hair spilled down her back, and pearly white scales shimmered in the fading light. She wore a ceremonial robe woven from seaweed, which draped around her arms as she lifted them toward the surface.

Tristan leaned toward me to whisper, "That's Sanvi. She's our spiritual leader."

We didn't have much for spiritual leaders back home. We believed in the gods who created us, but didn't worship them as other religions did. Instead, we had funeral directors to host memorials like this one, or officiants for wedding ceremonies, but these jobs weren't directly tied to spiritual practices. It was another way we differed from the Luna pod.

Sanvi used her sonic scream to project her voice over the crowd. "As the sun sets over the sea, we gather to honor the lives of our dear loved ones—Trenton Aberforth, Caspian Seaver, Zander Porpoise, Dylon Orman, Ronan Anchor, and a dear dolphin friend Delphina."

I clutched my shell closer to my chest. This was the first time I'd heard the names of Tristan's brothers. Though I hadn't known them, I felt for Tristan's loss. Hearing Delphina's name among them made that ache in my heart entirely personal.

Sanvi continued. "I now invite the families to approach the Ancestral Trench and offer up tokens of remembrance in the name of the departed, so that we may remember their bravery and strength, and their courage may live on in our hearts."

Dozens of people swam forward, and they took turns

giving a parting speech, before dropping their tokens into the trench. The families offered a variety of beautiful shells, colorful gems, ornate spears, and even seafood—anything that may have represented or belonged to the deceased. Each token seemed to float in the water for a moment, before slowly sinking to the depths of the trench. It was so beautiful, a symbolic goodbye.

A couple who looked to be in their fifties approached the trench. The man twisted a net of seaweed in his hands, while the woman trailed her fingers along the frame of a hand-held mirror.

"Our dearest Ronan," the man said. "I offer up this token of a sea net, in remembrance of your artistry. No one could weave a net quite like you, and no fish could ever escape it, for it was your expert hand that kept our bellies fed, but your passion, love, and creativity that fed our joy. We will remember you always."

The man tossed the net into the trench. When it was the woman's turn, she opened her mouth to speak, but it appeared she choked on seawater.

"Is she okay?" I whispered to Tristan.

"That is Ronan's mother," he explained. "It is common among seafolk to lose their voice when suffering a great tragedy, for there is a time to use our sonic scream, and a time to hold it close to our hearts. She will gain her voice back in time, but right now she can't speak."

I wondered if that's why my father and I could never quite say how we felt after my grandmother died. We'd been denied our sonic scream our whole lives, that in the deepest depths of our despair, we didn't know how to use our voice.

Ronan's mother dropped the mirror into the Ancestral Trench, and it gently flipped a few times before disappearing from view.

After the families paid their respects, Sanvi invited close friends to say their partings. Tristan led me forward, and we hovered over the edge of the trench. The friendship part of the ceremony was less formal than the family portion, because there were so many people gathered that we couldn't all take turns with speeches. Instead, seafolk spoke over one another and whispered prayers before dropping their tokens into the sea depths. It seemed the ceremony should be chaotic, but it wasn't. All the voices overlapping one another seemed to swell into a harmonious chorus, like a song.

Tristan reached into the sack he'd brought along and withdrew five tokens, one for each of his lost companions. "Trenton, I offer up this token of a fire agate, in symbolism of the passion and fire you brought to our friendship. That fire will live on, and the spark you started will never die out."

He dropped the stone into the trench, then continued. For Caspian, he offered a golden pearl to symbolize the sun and the bright, lively spirit of his friend. Zander received a silver coin in his name, as a sign of the abundance and good fortune he brought to all. For Dylon, he gave a compass, one that looked old and must've belonged to his friend, in remembrance of Dylon's adventurous nature. Finally, for

Ronan he gave a section of rope, twisted as expertly from seaweed as the net Ronan's father offered. It must've been crafted by Ronan's own hand. Tristan said the rope symbolized the bond the friends shared.

Next, it was my turn. I held the shell I'd collected over the trench, hesitating to let it go. Once I did, it would be gone forever, and with it, a piece of myself would drift downward into that trench, never to be retrieved again. "Delphina," I started, but I choked up.

"Take all the time you need," Tristan offered.

I drew a deep breath of sea water. I wasn't sure if I'd been beneath the surface too long, or my lungs just refused to work, because it didn't seem like enough breath to satisfy me. "Delphina, you were one of my closest friends..."

I could hardly get the words out. Then a gentle hand landed on my shoulder, and I turned to see Noah there.

"Delphina was kind, generous, and brave," he started as he stared into the depths below us. "She always made sure everyone on the beach was having a good time."

Noah had lived outside Sea Haven for the past year, so it hadn't occurred to me that he might've known Delphina before he left.

"She knew how to brighten anyone's day by performing tricks or taking people on rides out to sea," Noah continued. "She could always find the shiniest of rocks beneath the dullest sand bars. I offer this rock in memory of her, as a reminder of how she brought joy to us all."

Noah unfurled his hand, and a bright blue rock fell

from his palm and into the trench. My heart swelled at his kind words, which caused the lump in my throat to ease.

"She was wonderful," Liana agreed as she came up beside me. "I looked for a rock or shell that reminded me of her, but I couldn't find one that did her memory justice. So instead, I offer a song, much like the ones she used to sing."

Liana lifted her hands, and from out of the crowd, a group of dolphins swam over the trench. Together, they let out a series of clicks and whistles that echoed to the depths of the sea and back. Liana harmonized with them, and though there were no words to her song, I understood it completely.

Liana must've organized this with the dolphin pod. These dolphins hadn't known Delphina, but they sang a song of mourning to honor her.

Back in Sea Haven, we could feel the emotions of sea creatures, but we'd never been able to communicate with them to the depth of our ancestors. Now that we were far away from that awful sea stone, I could feel my magic awakening, because I *understood* the dolphin language, even if I couldn't translate it into words.

From deep within the trench, a low, rumbling note rang out. I peered over the edge and noticed movement below us, though I couldn't make out what it was.

"There's something down there," I whispered to Tristan.

"That's the Kraken," he explained. "He's an ancient being whom some say has been with the Luna pod since before Luna City formed. Our tokens are not just offers of remembrance, but symbols of our grief, which the Kraken consumes so that he can hold on to our memories for generations."

"That's beautiful," I told him.

The Kraken's song grew louder, crescendoing in harmony with Liana and the dolphin chorus. I noticed something different in my best friend's voice that I'd never heard before. It sounded as if her voice had multiple layers, all resonating together like a choir. The beautiful tone echoed to the bottom of the trench and back, filling my heart much like the siren song we'd heard at the island.

Tristan had been right. Merfolk shouldn't be alone when grieving. Having my friends here meant everything.

The song faded, and it was my turn.

I stepped up to the very edge of the drop-off. "I offer this shell to symbolize Delphina's pure intentions. She may not be here with us anymore, but her memory will live on."

I dropped the shell into the trench. A long orange tentacle covered in suction cups stretched upward, barely touching the light, as if the Kraken was reaching out to accept my offering. My heart swelled at the gesture. The darkness below suddenly didn't feel so hopeless and empty, but filled with blessings.

My shell disappeared into the shadows, and the Kraken's tentacle retreated out of sight. I turned to Liana, and we fell into each other's arms. After a long time, we finally drew away from one another.

"Thank you, Tristan, for including Delphina in the

ceremony," I said. "Noah, Liana, thank you both. Delphina would've loved this tribute."

Everyone else had finished their prayers, so we returned to our spots in the crowd. Cordelia was only a few feet away from us, and she placed a hand on Tristan's shoulder to rub it. She shot a dark glare in my direction, though I couldn't quite read it. It made me feel uncomfortable, but I wrote it off as a sign of her grief. Surely it was nothing personal.

Sanvi continued the ceremony, closing it out with a song that we all joined in on. The lyrics were in a language I didn't recognize, but I tried to keep up with the melody.

After the memorial was over, several people came up to Tristan to offer their condolences. I watched in awe at the respect he received from his pod. He took each of their hands in turn and bowed his head in gratitude. It was obvious these people held him in high esteem.

We followed the others back to the heart of the city, where a large feast had been set up in a big open area that Tristan told me was the town square. Since there were so many people who'd come to pay their respects, there wasn't a room in the palace big enough to host them all.

The town square was just as grand as the palace. A sandy seabed lay beneath us, while rock formations home to all colors of coral rose on all sides. Seafolk gathered around tables made from huge scallop shells and feasted on delicious oysters and wonderful shrimp. There was some sort of pudding for dessert that looked like it might be made from jellyfish. Around us, people laughed as they shared stories and celebrated the lives of those who'd passed.

Liana and Noah were at the buffet table with their guards, deep in a conversation about how the merfolk prepared and seasoned their food underwater. Cordelia and Zale had gone over to a table where guests were supplying a scale apiece from their own tails to attach to the inside of a giant mollusk shell, which Tristan said would be placed near the palace as a memorial. I thought that was amazing, because everyone who loved these people got to put a part of themselves into the monument. It was a lot to take it all in, and I looked around in wonder.

Tristan eyed me curiously. "You look intrigued. Is this different from your customs back home?"

"Yes and no," I said as I finished a bite of pudding. "We hold funerals and share stories just like this, but it always has a layer of sadness over it. Here, the stories feel more... lively. The memorial you're working together to create is beautiful. It seems you honor what you had, rather than focus on what you lost. It's really cool to see your community coming together like this."

Tristan's curious expression morphed into something else—compassion, perhaps?

He piqued my interest when he extended a hand in my direction. "Come with me. I want to show you something."

CHAPTER 5

Tristan and I swam far away from the town square, climbing toward the water's surface until we came upon a seamount at the edge of the city. It was like a tall underwater hill that appeared to be the remnants of an ancient volcano. The seamount was bare of any coral or ocean life, apart from a rather large octopus moving along the rock.

Tristan guided me to the top of the seamount, and I lowered myself through the water until my feet hit the rock and I was walking along the seafloor. A humpback whale and her calf swam leisurely overhead, singing a song that echoed off the seabed.

From here, I could see all the way to the end of the city far in the distance. The sun was setting now, casting the ocean in a dull green hue, but down in the city below us, bioluminescent algae lit up the ocean with a gorgeous array of colors. The glow of the algae ebbed and flowed with the gentle current.

Tristan swam up beside me to gaze out over the sea. "We call this place the Landing. It's where the first of the ancient pods stopped to rest, and when they looked out over the valley below, they knew this would be their new home. Over the following years, Luna City became widely known as a safe haven among merfolk who were being driven away from shore by humans. Merfolk from all over the world came here to start a new life."

Tristan held out a hand, gesturing for me to follow him. I took his hand and walked along the ocean floor until we came upon a large rock twice as tall as I was. Upon the face of the rock were inscriptions of different words in various handwritings.

I reached out to run my fingers over the carvings, reading them out in a whisper. *"We are Coral. We are Bathyal. We are Mackerel."*

My fingers trailed over other etchings that appeared to be in different languages. "What does all this mean?"

"These are the pods who came to Luna City hundreds of years ago," Tristan explained. "When new pods arrived, they came to the Landing to inscribe their pod's name on this rock, to remind us of where we came from. Many of these languages are still spoken here today, because even though we are one pod now, our experiences are shaped by our history and the lives and traditions of our ancestors. We believe that by honoring what has passed, we create connections for the future."

"This is amazing," I remarked. "That must be why your memorial song was in another language. There's such a rich history here."

Tristan nodded. "The Landing holds our history, just like the Kraken holds our hearts. The Landing reminds us that it is okay to feel sadness in the wake of tragedy, but we do not have to lose who we are to it. Sadness is something to express, not push aside. We know that with every loss, there is also something to gain. And so we honor what once was, but we also take those cherished memories and lessons with us into the future."

"That's an amazing perspective," I said. "But how do you apply it? Do you have to simply accept loss as it comes?"

"There are certain things you cannot change, and those are the experiences you must accept and allow to move through you like the ocean waves. But you also can't just let life happen to you without actively involving yourself in it," Tristan said. "Take a look at our ecosystem."

He gestured around the Landing, which was nothing but rock. The octopus I'd seen earlier was long gone.

"This seamount used to be thriving with ocean life, but our fish and other sea creature population has suffered since Ocean Rock began polluting our waters," Tristan continued. "We cannot just accept this lying down. That is why we must do something about it, and when we succeed we will be able to restore this ecosystem, in which it can thrive better than it ever has before."

I glanced around the Landing, trying to imagine what it looked like when the ocean life thrived upon this rock. I bet it was beautiful, just as the city below us. It was alarming how close we were to the city, and all the sea life here was gone. I didn't know how much time the Luna pod had before the algae in the city below us died off, and the rest of the ecosystem followed, but I knew it couldn't be much longer.

This city was so beautiful when we arrived, but there was darkness brewing beneath the surface, and I couldn't bear to witness these people losing anything more than they already had.

I turned back toward the city to look over the glowing landscape. Choral music drifted upward from the town square below as the memorial service continued.

"Their songs are so beautiful," I remarked.

"They are," he agreed. "Would you like to sing along?"

I nodded, and Tristan and I sat along the edge of the Landing, which dropped off like a cliff below us. Tristan began to hum to the tune, and his magic instantly began to soothe me with the power of his siren song.

The melody repeated, and I joined in on the song. I didn't sing any lyrics, because it was in another language I didn't know, but I allowed my voice to rise and fall to the tune the choir sang from below. Something wasn't quite right about it, though. Tristan's voice echoed with a resonance that seemed to stretch out far into the depths of the sea and back, blending in with the rest of the song even though the choir was far away from us. Though I sang the same notes, my tone seemed to clash with his, never quite blending as it should.

My voice cracked, and my fingers went to my throat when I realized what was happening. My words came out sounding hoarse. "I don't have my siren call."

Tristan furrowed his brow and dropped his gaze to my legs. "Just as you do not have your tail," he mused. "Perhaps there is a pattern to which powers you possess and which are suppressed."

"What if they're lost forever?" I worried.

Tristan shook his head firmly. "We can't assume that without giving it more time. You've already discovered your sonic scream, and so we must consider that your tail and siren call will appear in time as well. Have you noticed any other changes to your magic since leaving Sea Haven?"

"My control over the water feels stronger," I noted. "When the dolphins sang at the memorial, I felt a deeper connection to them, so I must be developing more abilities to communicate with sea life. I'd rather not test if I can breathe underwater indefinitely just yet."

"We should proceed with caution on that one," Tristan agreed with a light laugh.

He placed his hand on the rock beside me, barely brushing his finger against mine. My heart gave a start, but when I glanced in his direction, it appeared that he hadn't felt a thing. Being here with him and looking down upon the city felt magical, but something within me recoiled, as if I was afraid I might fall under the pod's enchantment myself.

Apprehensively, I looked back toward the city. As the slow melody continued, a group of merfolk joined hands and rose high into the open sea, spinning and swirling in a beautiful tribute dance. Cerulean scales shimmered in the fading light, and even from this distance the sight of Noah snapped me back to attention.

I pulled my hand away from Tristan's. "Thank you for bringing me here. You've given me a lot to think about."

"Of course," he replied kindly. "It's important to know where you came from, so you can see where you're going."

The song began to fade, and we figured it was time to head back. By the time we arrived in the town square, the choir had finished, the tables were cleared, and folks were beginning to head back home.

A few people were still gathered, including Noah, Liana, and their mentors. Prince Zale was here too, twisting together various seashells with strands of seaweed. Liana watched him with bright eyes, until Zale finished and placed his creation atop her head like a crown. She gave a girlish giggle as she marveled at her reflection in the surface of a pearly shell.

A guard holding a trident swam in front of us. "Prince Tristan, the king has requested your presence."

"Yes, of course," Tristan said, before turning to me. "I'm afraid this is where I must leave you."

"I can find my own way back," I told him.

"Very well." He nodded. "I'll come get you in the morning, and we can begin training then."

Tristan swam off with the guard, and I headed toward my friends.

Liana's eyes caught mine, and she swam over to nudge me in the side. She wiggled her eyebrows. "Where'd you and Tristan sneak off to?"

I bumped shoulders with her, rolling my eyes. "It's not like that. Tristan was showing me some of Luna City's history."

Liana spread her arms wide, swaying her golden tail to spin herself in a circle. "This city is magical, isn't it? I don't think I can ever go back."

I frowned. This place was wonderful, beyond my wildest dreams, but Liana was acting like this was some fantasy vacation and not like we'd been forced to flee. "Li, we're here to help our people."

"That doesn't mean we can't enjoy this place while we're here." She shot a glance at Zale, then winked at me. "The prince is pretty cute, isn't he?"

"I guess so," I said, before playfully adding, "though he's no Dean Winchester."

Liana chuckled at our inside joke. "That's the Bree I know. The fact is, we're here whether we like it or not. We might as well make the most of it, and maybe your powers will turn up in the process."

I nearly winced. She was trying to stay positive like she always did, but it couldn't lift my spirits in the midst of all that happened. If Liana was content to look at the brighter side of life, that was fine, but I couldn't pretend as if there wasn't something dangerous lurking in the shadows.

"All right, go have fun with your prince," I encouraged, nudging her back in Zale's direction.

Liana glanced toward Noah, who was making his way toward us. She lowered her voice and whispered, "Looks like I'm not the only one who will be having fun tonight."

She bumped her shoulder into mine, then swam off toward Zale, leaving me alone with Noah.

Noah furrowed his brow. "What's up with her?"

I waved my hand nonchalantly. "She's just having fun. All those years playing mermaid at Sea Haven Beach were more like *preparation* than fairytales."

Noah glanced around at the towering rocks, which were glowing brighter with algae as the surface turned to night overhead. "It feels like a dream, I'll give her that. I can't believe I get to stay overnight in a sea palace. Have you seen the sleeping quarters yet? They're magnificent."

"I can't breathe underwater all night," I said. "I'm going back to the boat to get some sleep there."

"I'll swim you back to the surface," Noah offered.

It'd be nice having his company on the way back in the dark, and Noah could swim a lot faster than I could on my own.

"I'd like that," I said.

Liana was wrapped up in watching Zale weave another crown, so she waved us off and said goodnight.

I climbed onto Noah's back, and my shoulders relaxed against his warm skin.

"Hang on tight," he said.

Then Noah swished his fins through the water and took off toward the surface.

CHAPTER 6

Noah and I returned to the boat in the calm lagoon, and his fins transformed back into legs once we were on deck. The sun had set by now, and moonlight glimmered off the water.

My clothes were soaked, and I shivered slightly. "Thank you for swimming me back."

"Of course, I'm here to help," he offered. "Speaking of... hold on."

Noah ducked into the cabin and came back a moment later with a pile of dry clothes for me. "I found these earlier in one of the drawers. The t-shirt's probably a bit big for you, but it's dry."

My cheeks warmed as I took the clothes from him. "Thank you. I'll just be a minute."

I entered the cabin, which had a small kitchenette, a seating area around a table, and separate rooms for the bedroom and the bathroom. I slipped into a t-shirt and sweatpants, then found a blanket in the cabinet over the bed.

As I began climbing the stairs, I heard Noah humming a soft tune. His song seemed to echo like Liana's did when she sang at the Ancestral Trench, and the melody resonated through me like soft waves. I realized what I was feeling was the power of a siren's song pulsing through his voice. It was beautiful.

Noah was sitting on the bench in the back of the boat, but he stood when I returned, running his fingers through his hair. "If you're all settled in, then I'll head back to my quarters at the palace."

"Actually," I said quickly, stopping him. I didn't want him to leave. "You're welcome to stay for a bit, if you'd like."

His features softened, and a light smile touched his lips. "I saw some fishing gear in the boat. Let's see who can catch the biggest fish."

"You're on," I agreed.

We gathered the fishing gear and cast our lines into the water. I curled up on the bench beneath my blanket as we waited for something to bite.

Noah sat near me on the opposite end of the bench. "What do you think of Luna City?"

I kept my eyes on the moonlight dancing across the water's surface. "It's beautiful, but it's a lot to take in."

"It's different from back home," Noah agreed. "I never could've imagined a place like this still existed."

"Or that we'd ever have access to more magic," I added. I thought of Noah's cerulean scales and asked, "What was it like summoning your tail for the first time?"

He slowly reeled in his line. "Remember when we found our cores in the vials at City Hall, and you just *knew* which one was yours because you were drawn to it? It was kind of like that, just this deep inner knowing that can't be put into words. You'd think it'd be this big magical moment, but it just felt natural. But at the same time, it felt like a piece of me clicked into place that I've been searching for forever."

"I heard you humming earlier," I remarked. "You have your siren call, don't you?"

"I suppose I do." Noah cast his line out again. "I wasn't sure I would at first, but when the choir started singing, I joined in and it felt like I'd been singing that song my whole life."

I snuggled deeper under my blanket. "I'm glad it's coming so easily to you."

"You'll get it, too," Noah encouraged. "I know you will."

He nudged his foot against mine playfully, and the remaining tension I'd been holding on to melted away. It was easy to let go here with him, under a blanket of stars and the tranquility of the lagoon.

I smiled. "Thank you, Noah. For everything. You dropped everything in your old life to bring me back to Sea Haven. You didn't have to do that."

"I wanted to," Noah countered. "The day you showed up at my door was the first time I felt hope since I left home. I thought there might be something better out there for me after my parents passed, but I realize now I was just running away, and you gave me something worth running *toward*. I think in my heart I always knew there was more out there than Sea Haven had to offer, but I wasn't looking in the right places. Now that we're here with the Luna pod, I know there's more for us. I really believe we can bring this all back to our people."

"Changing everything about the way we grew up is a lot to expect of ourselves," I said. "As wonderful as Luna City is, there's a part of me that thinks things would be easier if we forgot what's happened and everything went back to the way it was."

Noah tilted his head curiously. "You don't seem like the kind of person to be afraid of change."

I scoffed as I fiddled with my reel. "Everyone thinks I'm this girl who likes getting into mischief, but the truth is mischief finds me and I'm terrified every time. I go along with stuff because I don't know how to say no. I question everything I do, but I'm not brave enough to face the answers. I don't have plans. I don't know what I'm doing or where I'm going, so I make rash decisions because maybe if I actually do it I won't be so scared. I make up scenarios in my head and let my dreams guide me because when I try to reason, I get stuck. I get bored easily, but I also don't like conflict. I'll do silly things like pull pranks, but when it comes to the hard stuff, I don't know how to handle it."

"If you need help working it out, I'm always here to talk," Noah offered. "You must've had some sort of plan for your future."

"I always saw myself growing old in Sea Haven," I admitted. "I assumed I'd get married and buy a house on the beach where I could share the ocean with the people I loved. All the other details didn't matter, because I figured life would unfold as it happened. Everyone wanted me to declare a major before school started, but I'm undecided because I don't know enough to make a big decision like that yet."

Noah nodded like he understood. "Have you ever given yourself the chance to consider other possibilities?"

I shrugged. "How can I know what I want when I don't know what my options are? I thought I had more time. My plan was to go to college and figure it out as I went, but I can't do that anymore. Problem is, I don't have the tools, knowledge, or expertise to figure out these problems we're currently facing."

"The Luna pod has offered to help us," Noah reminded me.

"Yes, but I don't know if I'm cut out for this. I've never fought these kinds of fights, and the Luna pod wants to make us into some sort of warriors. How can I commit to that when I don't know anything about these people?"

"Do you think it's better not knowing what's out there and just doing what you're told?"

"It'd be easier, but I don't think that makes it *better*. I thought I was happy. I thought Sea Haven was the best place in the world. But that illusion has been shattered. I want peace for everyone, but I don't think true peace can exist where lies and deception persist, because those lies are designed to rob us of our full potential. Growing up in a bubble meant never striving for more, or exploring solutions that could actually help other people. How many secrets back home are being kept behind closed doors, and I never even thought about it because I was told everything was fine and blindly believed it?"

"Everything is not fine," Noah said. "Sea Haven looks great on the surface, because everyone's content to pretend things are wonderful, but they keep quiet when real issues arise. There are a lot of people in Sea Haven struggling, and everyone's happy to sweep it under the rug because they don't want to mess up their perfect vision of paradise. After my parents died, the community should've been there for me and provided support, but instead they threw me out the second they had a chance. It's not your fault that you didn't see it for what it was."

"I chose not to see it, though. When I found you, I was so focused on getting back home, as if I could go back to the way things were, but I didn't even look around Illinois and try to experience what the rest of the world was like. I should've been more willing to look outside myself, but I was just being selfish."

Noah shook his head. "I don't think it was selfish of you to want to take back what was stolen from you."

"I guess you're right," I mused. "But even though I got my magic back, it's not what I expected. When I lost my core, it was like losing a piece of myself, and now that I have it back, it's not the same. Getting my magic back didn't fix everything, and now we're here in a place we don't belong. Sea Haven was supposed to be my future, and now without it I don't know where to go. I don't know... maybe my core was damaged when they took it and that's why I can't summon my tail."

Noah shook his head. "You'll never convince me Carson Ray has the power to fracture a person's core. He's a lying piece of crap, but he's arrogant enough to take credit for something like that, and he never did."

"I suppose that's true." I sighed. "I don't think I can fully comprehend the lie because I don't know anything else, and I need more life experience before I can understand it and put any of it into perspective. I think that's why we aren't allowed out of Sea Haven, because if we don't know any better, who's to question it? Our real selves are being suppressed, and I think that's one of the worst things a person can do to someone else."

"I think you know who you are, deep down," Noah encouraged. "But all those parts are intertwined with these lies, and now you've got to untangle it all and figure out which parts are *you*, and which parts are someone else's belief system imposed upon you."

"Where do I start?" I asked.

"What do you *know* to be true about yourself—something that Carson Ray and all the other Sea Haven Council members could never strip away from you?"

I thought about it for a moment. "I think I'm good at seeing the best in people, which is why being exiled was so hard, because I believed that people were better than that. And I still believe most people are good people, but when you're hurt by the people who are supposed to take care of you, it makes you question everything."

"I can understand that," Noah agreed.

"I know that I'm loyal," I added. "I love my family and friends, and nothing the Sea Haven Council could do would make me abandon them."

"Bree Waters, Loyal Friend," Noah noted with a smile. "You know where to start now, because that loyalty lies within your heart. It's not going to be easy, but now you get to peel back the layers and decide which parts of you that you want to keep, and which you want to toss away."

"I think that's what's difficult," I realized. "When you're told who you are and what to be, you can just go along without question. Now the choice is up to me, and I have to decide—do I want to be the girl I was brought up to be with her power limited, or can I become the mermaid I was born to be?"

"Is it even a question?"

"If I'm completely honest, Noah, I'm afraid of what this power makes me and who I could become, but most of all, I wonder what parts of myself I have to lose in the process," I said. "It's scary to think that if I have all this power, I could do something great with it. When you've been kept small your whole life, greatness is terrifying, because now I have the chance to become something greater than I ever thought was possible."

"I can understand that. Back home, things just *happened* to me, and I went along with it. Remember how I told you I was charged with vandalism, and that's why I left? It wasn't my idea to graffiti the lighthouse. My friends dragged me along that night, but when the cops arrived, I was the one who was caught, stripped of my magic, and shipped off. I didn't even try to plead my case, because I didn't want my friends to get in trouble. Then you showed up with this opportunity to take the reins on my life for the first time, and now look where we are. The world has opened up to us, and now *we* get to decide what we want."

"Yeah, we do!" I agreed. "I may not know where to start, but I know how I want this to end. When Carson sent me away, I remember thinking it was fine if he took Sea Haven away from me, as long as I had my magic, but that was a lie. Sea Haven will always be my home. I don't *want* to leave it behind. My dad kept saying we'll figure this all out, and then I could come back home, and you know what? I still believe that."

"So you want to save Sea Haven?" Noah's voice rose hopefully.

I nodded. "It's unfair that we had to leave because someone else said so. That's *our* town, and no one can take it from us. Our perfect vision of home may be shattered, but we can still put the pieces back together and make it better than ever before. After we help the Luna pod, I'm going back, exposing the council for their corruption, and ridding Sea Haven of its secrets and lies. We'll restore our people's full access to magic, and then Sea Haven will know *true* peace and freedom. But to do that, I need to unlock my powers. I have to learn who I am and not who I've been told to be, even if the girl I used to be was the safe option."

"We'll figure it out. Together." Noah leaned forward and held up a pinky. His eyes sparkled like the stars above us. "Promise?"

The air grew warmer between us, and I knew I could trust him. Noah and I came from the same world, and he understood exactly what I was going through. I was really glad to have him here. Liana understood to some degree, but I didn't think she could truly comprehend the depths of what we were up against because she hadn't had her core stripped away. She didn't know what it felt like to be without it.

I smiled, then looped my pinky around Noah's. "I pinky promise."

Noah and I laughed, but he cut off when he felt a tug on his line. He reeled in a fish as long as his arm, with sparkly scales and a big mouth. I held up my fingers and pretended to take a picture while he showed off his fish, and we laughed again.

This felt like the real me, someone who cared so deeply that she'd stop at nothing to get what she wanted. Maybe I didn't know how this would all play out, but I knew one thing for certain. Once I uncovered the rest of my powers, I could fully step into the woman I needed to be, and the path ahead would be clear.

I just worried about what I might have to sacrifice in the process.

CHAPTER 7

When I woke the next morning, the sun was peeking up over the island, and birds were beginning to sing their songs of daybreak. Noah had returned to the palace after our conversation last night, but it'd been nice having him here. He helped talk me down, and I felt like I finally had my head on straight.

I sat on the deck of the boat, twisting my hair into a braid as I watched schools of fish darting around in the crystal-clear waters below me. A group of tiny silver fish twisted among the coral, but one of them bumped into a rock and got turned around. When he righted himself, the rest of the school was gone, and he swam in circles looking for them.

"Aw, poor little guy," I muttered.

I used my magic to connect with the fish and felt his anxiety moving through me. He started in the opposite direction of his school, obviously completely lost.

"It's okay," I told him as I leaned over the side of the boat to touch the water. Magic pulsed from my fingertips, rippling through the lagoon until I connected with the fish. I used my powers to communicate with him. "Your school is just over there, behind that colony of coral."

The fish turned around, following my directions until he spotted the other fish and darted over to them, falling into sync beside them. A deep sense of gratitude filled my chest, and I heard a *Thank you* in my mind. There were no distinct words, yet it was as clear as if someone had spoken the phrase aloud.

It caught me off guard at first, because while I'd always had the ability to communicate with sea life to a degree, I'd never received such a direct message. I knew that meant my powers must be growing.

I withdrew my fingers from the water, amazed at how much deeper my connection to the sea already felt.

"You're improving already, Bree," a deep voice said from my right. I startled and peered over the side of the boat to see Tristan floating nearby, pushing long blond strands of hair from his eyes. Water droplets dripped from his beard and clung to his muscled shoulders, and his green tail glistened in the morning sun. Tristan rolled onto his back and swished his tail to glide through the water in front of me. "We'll be swimming races before sundown."

I crinkled my nose and gestured down to my legs. "Unless you can teach me how to summon my tail by the end of the day, I'm not bringing home any trophies."

I thought of my trophy back home that I'd won in the Sea Festival swimming contest a few years ago. I'd trained so hard for that and had been so proud of my performance, but I'd be much faster with a tail.

"As long as you're putting in the effort, you're a winner to me." Tristan smacked his fins on the surface of the water. "Come along. We don't want to be late for breakfast."

I dove into the lagoon, enjoying the cool, refreshing sensation as the water surrounded me. Tristan plunged beneath the surface and swished his fins until he was in front of me. His tail was so powerful that I was rocked by his wake. I started swimming, trying to keep up, but I wasn't even close.

He shot a glance over his shoulder. "You're like a little seahorse," he teased.

I rolled my eyes. Seahorses were well known as some of the slowest fish in the sea. "That's just unfair."

He shrugged. "But is it true?"

"It's true," I grumbled.

He laughed lightly. "Hold on tight, seahorse!"

I curled my arms around his shoulders, and he took off out of the lagoon.

We reached Luna City in no time, and Tristan led me

to the royal palace, where the guards moved aside to let us pass through the main entrance. The prince guided me down the main corridor, then turned down a wide hall I hadn't seen the last time I'd been here. Chatter grew louder as we approached a chamber at the end of the corridor.

We entered an expansive room with a long dining table that stretched from one end of the room to the other. Intricately carved stone chairs surrounded the table, and over a dozen merfolk were already passing shell plates filled to the brim with seafood around. High above our heads, a glass domed ceiling allowed sunlight to filter in through the water, filling the chamber with a turquoise glow. A bloom of jelly fish swam over the glass, adding to the wonder of the exquisite room.

"This is the royal dining quarters. It's where the royal family, the king's council, and our guests eat." Tristan gestured with an open hand. "You're welcome here any time of day. Choose any seat you'd like."

I took a moment to observe the room, and I noticed Liana and Noah among the merfolk at the far end of the table. Liana sat next to her mentor, Maren, and looked to be in a deep conversation with Prince Zale on the other side of her. She was talking about how our plates were flatter back home and we didn't need to worry about our food floating off if it was too buoyant. The young prince's eyes sparkled with intrigue.

Meanwhile, Noah was on the other side of the table, floating before Lamar, who was dressed in a golden breastplate that complemented his emerald-green scales. Lamar held up an intricate spear with a dark green rock carved to a point on the end. Noah looked over his mentor's weapon carefully.

"Give it a try," Lamar offered, handing Noah the spear. "See how you handle it."

Beside them, Cordelia observed as Noah spun the spear in his hands, testing its weight. Then Noah lunged forward, aiming the tip straight at the center of Lamar's breastplate.

The merman laughed as the spear made the tiniest of *clinks* against the armor. "You'll get the hang of it," Lamar said. "We'll practice more after breakfast."

Noah gave the spear back, and the two of them returned to their seats.

"The spear is too long for him," Cordelia said thoughtfully. "I should have one that will suit Noah better. You two should stop by The Marina this afternoon after your training."

Noah's eyes lit up. "Really? That'd be great!"

Tristan took the open seat beside Cordelia, while I sat on the opposite side of him, placing myself between Tristan and Noah. I should've known better, because their proximity brought an unexpected heat to rise in my stomach. I nibbled on shrimp but found my focus drifting quickly from my appetite.

"Luna City has a marina?" I asked to ease the tension in my gut.

"The Marina is Cordelia's store," Tristan explained.

"Oh, you own a shop?" I asked her.

She crinkled her nose, like she thought I was trying to insult her, which was the furthest thing from the truth. On the contrary, I was impressed. In Sea Haven, it was quite an accomplishment for someone our age to run a successful business.

"Nobility have very important jobs around here, and my business is more than just a *shop*," Cordelia insisted. "I'm an artist. I design and build weapons like Lamar's spear, which I made with my own hands."

"That's really cool that you already know what you want to do with the rest of your life," I remarked.

Cordelia raised her chin. "Yes, well, some of us know *exactly* what we want and will fight to keep it."

My spine straightened at her hostility. I'd intended for it to be a compliment because I admired her drive to go after what she wanted. Instead, I felt as if she'd jabbed that spear in my back. It was obvious she was not interested in a *surface dweller* inhabiting her city, and my legs were a stark reminder that I didn't belong here.

"That makes us both fighters," I stated curtly, before turning to Noah. "What do you need a spear for?"

Cordelia bristled, but I seemed to be the only one who noticed.

Noah swallowed a scallop. "Lamar wants to get me fitted for armor and begin training with the military academy here in Luna City. They need all the manpower they can get if Ocean Rock attacks."

"We haven't had to use our military forces for over a

century," Lamar added. "But since Ocean Rock arrived, we've reopened the academy and have been training as many soldiers as we can. I just hope we can negotiate reasonably before we witness another massacre."

"I'll help with that any way I can," Noah offered.

"Even the smallest details are helpful," Maren said. "Liana has been telling me stories of the surface that have already provided great insight to how humans operate."

Liana set her fork aside. "It's a whole different world on the surface! Can you believe the Luna Pod has never heard the lyrics to *Bohemian Rhapsody*?"

Noah rubbed his chin. "That's interesting, considering some fans think Freddie Mercury was a siren himself."

Liana's eyes lit up. "Do you really think so?"

"Freddie Mercury was *not* a siren," I said.

"It's possible he had some merfolk blood in him!" Liana raved.

"What's this song you speak of?" Zale wondered. "I'll have to give it a listen."

"I can give you a whole list of songs to listen to and movies to watch!" Liana exclaimed. "I'm a theater geek, so I'm going to start you off with some of the *best* musicals."

Zale kept his unblinking eyes on her, giddy with excitement as he became engrossed in her recommendations. She rambled a million miles per minute, giving the prince a run-down of her favorite shows and artists. I didn't know how Zale processed it all, but he seemed to hang on her every word and nodded along eagerly.

King Aalto entered the dining hall, flanked by two

guards who joined him at the head of the table. A chair remained empty beside him, which I could only assume was reserved for the queen.

The king's eyes fell upon his youngest son, and he frowned. "Zale, what are you still doing here?"

"Liana was just telling me about customs on the surface," Zale replied innocently. "It's all very useful information."

"It's not useful if they notice you missing from the drillship and your absence exposes us all," King Aalto said in a commanding tone. "You've been gone too long."

Liana glanced between the royals. "What do you mean?"

"I've been living undercover on Ocean Rock's ship for a while now, trying to gather information that will help in our negotiations," Zale explained. "I report back to Luna City weekly to share what I've learned. Father's right. I should've been back by now, and so I must take my leave."

Zale took Liana's hand and placed a gentle kiss on the back of it. "It was wonderful to meet you. Until we meet again."

Liana snickered as Zale bowed his head, then swam off.

I turned to the king. "Has Zale been able to learn anything that's helpful to the pod?"

He began filling his plate. "We've learned some about how they operate, but viewing it through the lens of seafolk is not helpful in truly understanding humans and the way they think. From a merfolk's point of view, we are one with the sea and would never seek to harm it, and so Ocean Rock's motivations make little sense to us. We would rather seek to uplift our community rather than destroy it."

King Aalto cleared his throat. "Even in the midst of this conflict, we must maintain connections with our own community. After breakfast, I will be speaking at the art gallery's opening ceremony for a new exhibit. You are all welcome to join, if you can spare a few hours from your training."

The invitation to an art exhibit got me excited. It sounded fun and spontaneous, and sea art was right up my alley, but then I recalled my conversation with Noah last night. Going to the art gallery would be fun, but it'd take time away from my training.

My gaze flickered in Noah's direction, and his eyes locked on mine. He raised his eyebrows slightly, not to sway me in one direction or the other, but to ask, *Which are you going to choose?*

The old me would've chosen the fun option, delaying my duty and giving little thought to building my future. Look where that'd gotten me—exiled from my home with no access to my siren song or mertail. I could either stay comfortable where I was at, or put in the work to become something more.

It was the most intimidating choice I'd been faced with yet, because I was out of place here, didn't know the people or the rules, and yet was expected to do something when I didn't know how to help. I told Cordelia I was a fighter, but I wasn't sure I wanted to become a warrior. Even so, I couldn't make that choice without having all the information laid out in front of me. I had to train so that I could learn more of what was required of me, and understand what the Luna pod was asking me to do.

"Thank you for the invitation," I told the king. "I'd love to be there, but I need to focus on my training."

Maybe it wasn't the choice Noah expected me to make, but it was a step in the right direction. If I was going to form a plan on how to defeat the Sea Haven Council, I needed information first, and so I had to learn as much as I could from these people.

No matter how long it took.

CHAPTER 8

Tristan and I left the dining hall to begin our first training session.

"Where will we be training?" I asked as we swam back toward the entrance to the palace.

"It's a surprise," he replied with a playful smirk. He slowed outside the palace entrance and shot a glance over his shoulder. "Hop on, little seahorse."

I shook my head at the nickname. "You're not going to let that one die, are you?"

He grinned. "Not if it continues to make you smile."

I rolled my eyes to hide my widening grin. I wrapped my arms around his shoulders to climb on his back.

Tristan swished his fins, and we took off toward the ocean's surface. The city appeared as a colorful blur below us, before it was gone from our sight entirely. Bubbles tickled my skin as we moved through the water effortlessly. My heart hammered in exhilaration. It felt like a dream to be able to swim this fast.

The ocean floor began to rise up as we entered shallower waters. A huge wall of rock rose before us, but Tristan aimed for a large hole big enough for multiple merfolk to fit through at once. Darkness enveloped us as we entered a tunnel. I clung to him tighter as he navigated around twists and turns in the cave.

I let out a small yelp that turned into a laugh. "Tristan, where are we going?"

"I told you, it's a surprise. Close your eyes."

I squeezed my eyes shut tightly, and before I knew it, Tristan slowed and our heads broke the surface of the water. Warm sunlight kissed my cheeks, and I let go of him to float through the water on my own.

"You can open them now," he said.

I peeled my eyes open, and my breath caught when I witnessed the beauty of the island surrounding us. Tristan had led me to a large, stunning cove surrounded on three sides by tall cliffs and green foliage. Sunlight danced through the clear blue waters, and beyond the opening to the cove, ocean waves swelled but never reached this quiet sanctuary.

I turned to take it all in. My jaw hung slack when I saw a gorgeous waterfall flowing through the center of it all, cascading down from the cliffside in multiple streams that glistened in the morning light.

"Tristan, it's beautiful," I said breathlessly.

"It really is," he replied without taking his eyes off me. "Welcome to Crystal Cove. I thought we could start our training by getting you acquainted with these waters. The stronger your connection with the sea, the greater your power will be. Come on."

Tristan gestured to me to follow him, then dove beneath the water again. I ducked my head below the surface, inhaling a deep breath of salt water. I understood why this place was called Crystal Cove, because the waters were crystal clear. I could see perfectly in all directions.

Tristan shot me a smirk. "Try to keep up."

All I saw was the glint of his green scales and a mass of bubbles where he'd just been, and then he was gone.

"Hey!" I called with a laugh, my sonic scream echoing throughout the cove.

Tristan's laughter rang back, but he was already far ahead of me. I pushed my arms through the water, pulling myself up beside him.

"Look at that!" Tristan pointed out a manta ray, and I slowed to observe the creature's majestic movements. "Over there!"

I turned to see an eel slithering between the rocks.

The cove was brimming with ocean life. Tristan continued on, pointing out interesting sea creatures and beautiful shells. I picked up a long, spiral seashell with an intricate pattern and set it aside to take back to the boat later.

Tristan darted forward. "Come check this out!"

He was halfway across the cove before I even looked up. It occurred to me then what Tristan was doing. He was trying to get me to keep up with him, to see if my tail would appear if I pushed myself to swim harder. Determination rose within me. Tail or not, he didn't know how competitive I could be, and if he wanted to race, he was *on*.

Summoning my power, I commanded the sea to rise up, then ordered the water to propel me forward. I reached Tristan on the other side of the cove in moments, but he was already swishing his fins and pulling away.

"Oh, no you don't," I called. I ordered the water to push me forward, and I shot out in front of him. I pulled ahead a few inches, before the two of us moved in an arc around the edge of the cove. We were nearly touching as I tried to block him, but he took the lead anyway.

Tristan shot a smirk over his shoulder. "Oh, yes, I *do*. Eat my bubbles!"

He swam in front of me, playfully swaying his fins, which caused a cloud of bubbles to fill my vision. I commanded a stream of water to push between them, but when the bubbles cleared, Tristan was gone. I wondered if I'd gained the lead, until I heard his laughter coming from beneath me.

I looked down to see Tristan swimming on his back, his arms propped nonchalantly above his head. He smiled mischievously. "You can swim faster than that, can't you?"

"Go ahead, mock me, fish boy," I teased. I thrust a stream of water in his direction, but he dodged it.

Tristan flicked his fins, pushing himself upright. "Fish boy? Better to be a fish than a seahorse!"

Tristan swam in an arc above me, literally *swimming circles* around me. It didn't matter how fast I commanded the water to push me forward because Tristan's tail gave him a huge advantage.

I slowed and crossed my arms. "How about you get rid of that tail of yours and then we'll see who's faster?"

Tristan lifted his hands in surrender. "All right, we'll even the playing field."

His green scales morphed into pants, and he treaded water.

"First one out of the cove is the *real* seahorse," I joked as I kicked off a rock.

From behind me, Tristan grabbed my leg and yanked me back. He quickly pushed ahead of me. I yelped and grabbed his shoulders to keep him from pulling ahead, but he kept kicking his legs and dragging me along. Our laughter echoed from one end of the cove and back.

"Hey, what's that!?" I cried, pointing behind him.

Tristan turned, and I took the opportunity to push off of him and swim further ahead. "Not fair!" he called.

I kicked faster, pumping my arms through the water as I raced Tristan out of the cove. I swam as fast as I could, my heart racing and my breaths shallow. I sensed Tristan far behind me when I reached the edge of the island.

I flipped over to gloat, but Tristan was nowhere to be

seen. Then a tap came on my shoulder. I whirled around to see Tristan grinning at me and swaying his green scales through the water.

I shoved his shoulder lightly. "That's cheating."

"I'm not cheating. I'm *assessing*. Let's see how far you can take your magic," he suggested. "Show me your biggest wave."

"All right." I summoned my powers and felt my magic becoming one with the water below me. Energy surged upward, and my powers pushed Tristan and me to the surface, climbing a cresting wave that must've risen over fifty feet above the ocean's surface.

"Nice!" Tristan called.

I pushed myself higher, until only my feet were submerged in the water and we were surfing the peak of the wave toward a sandy beach. Exhilaration filled my chest, making my heart hammer. I'd never ridden a wave so large before.

The wave crashed onto the beach, and Tristan and I went rolling across the sand. He landed flat on his back and didn't move. I rushed over to him, only to find a grin spread across his face.

Tristan shot upright to a sitting position. "Let's do that again!"

Tristan and I rode three more waves, each one bigger than the last. He kept trying to get me to do different things with the waves, twisting them into columns or making shapes out of the water to test my precision. We must've been at it for hours before we returned to the cove.

"Bree, check this out!" Tristan waved me over, and I followed him around a large rock to find a sea turtle swimming toward us.

"She's magnificent," I said as I swam closer to her.

The sea turtle had a bit of seaweed on her head, so I reached out to help her. She reared her head upward. *Put it back*, she communicated with me.

"I think she wants to wear it as a hat," Tristan laughed.

I snickered as I placed the seaweed back on the turtle's head. She gave us a polite nod, then floated off. "She seems to have no care in the world."

"As should we," Tristan said. "It is in our nature to move with the rise and fall of the tides, and to flow with the ocean current."

"Unless you're caught in the center of a storm," I pointed out.

"Ah, but that is why we possess the power to cultivate them, in order to protect ourselves." Tristan winked. "Would you like to try?"

"You want me to control a storm?" I looked up at the sky, which was mostly clear except for a few sparse clouds.

Tristan held his hand in my direction. "No, Bree. I want you to *create* one."

CHAPTER 9

I'd never created or commanded a storm before, as that was one of the powers the council's sea stone had taken from me. I wanted to see what I could do.

I took Tristan's hand, and he led me to a large, flat rock at the edge of the cove. The rock was submerged in less than two feet of water, with gentle waves lapping over it. Other rocks jutted up out of the sea in an arc, creating a pool-like area we could sit in.

Tristan leaned his back against the rocks, propping his muscular arms up on either side of him. He lifted his chin toward the sun while curling his fins out of the water and back down again.

"I thought we were going to command a storm," I said.

Tristan drew a deep breath of ocean air. "The sea cannot be *commanded*, Bree. You must work with her. Sit, and see if you can feel what she feels."

I sat beside Tristan and closed my eyes. The water was calm here, but I still felt the gentle rise and fall of the waves moving across the beach not far from here.

"Do you feel that?" he asked.

"Yes," I told him. "I feel her moving and swaying, like a gentle dance, and I can almost feel her... inviting me in, like she wants me to dance with her."

"That's exactly it!" Tristan said proudly. "You're worried you've lost too much of your magic, but that connection you have to the sea is still within you. The humans think they can just *take* whatever they want, but merfolk await an invitation and make the most of their calling. You sense that invitation because you are a merfolk through and through, Bree. Now, will you accept her dance?"

I nodded. "Yes."

"Then move with the sea to build this storm," Tristan instructed. "Transmute this energy you feel into something bigger and bolder."

"How do I do that?" I wondered.

"The ocean holds all the power of the sea at any given time," Tristan explained. "Here on the surface, the water is calm, but if you connect deeply enough with her, you will find a raging torrent brewing somewhere beneath the surface. It is your job to connect with the energy in which you want to summon, and bring it forth."

I waited for a minute, assessing the energy of the sea around me. At first, all I felt was the gentle flow of water across my skin, but the deeper I dug, the stronger I sensed the waves swelling and retreating from shore. I didn't use my powers just yet to change anything, but expanded my reach even further, observing what my magic could find.

I reached far into the depths of the sea, until I could sense the smallest currents rippling off the sea life around me. Miles away, I felt the rush of water growing deep in the ocean's depths.

"There's already a storm coming," I realized.

Tristan nodded. "Yes. Now that you've found it, you can draw that energy to you, and the sea will handle the rest."

"All right, I'll give it a shot." I focused my magic on the energy pulsing somewhere far away from us. My connection with the sea ran deep, and I attempted to speak to her through my intention, similar to the way I communicated with the sea life. I remained calm, requesting her assistance as if I could coax a storm out of her with kindness. Once I felt confident in my connection, I yanked the power toward me.

The waves swelled up around us, and I knew it must be working. I tugged harder, but my connection broke, and my magic came springing back into me like a slingshot. I gasped as a huge wave crested over top of us, crashing over mine and Tristan's heads and slamming us into the rock.

The wave receded, and I was pulled several feet from where I'd been sitting. I scowled and rubbed my elbow where I'd hit it.

Tristan pushed his hair out of his eyes. "That's a good start, but you can't command it nor resist it."

I nodded. "Right. I have to dance with it. Let me try again."

I resituated myself on the rocks, then closed my eyes to concentrate. I tried again, reaching my magic out for miles until I sensed the energy building deep in the sea. I didn't pull on it right away, but instead took my time to feel into it. The longer I sat there, the more I noticed that the raging currents felt familiar. Though the ocean was calm here on the surface, there was a part of her brewing with an anger that wanted to be released.

I tapped into that, feeling my own frustration rise within me like an incoming tide. The ocean seemed to resonate with me, and I realized it wasn't about manipulating her energy alone, but that she would respond to me, too. I took it as an invitation to bring that anger we shared to the surface. For once, I didn't stuff it down until it exploded out of me. I let it come at its own pace.

Images began to flash behind my lids, pictures of my family and friends back home who'd been left behind. I thought of my mother's fallen features when she found out I was leaving Sea Haven for college, and felt the ache in my chest because I was mad the council had forbidden me from telling her the truth. I pictured Christina's bright eyes meeting mine as I met up with her on Sea Haven Beach, and I gritted my teeth because I'd been forced to say goodbye to one of my dearest friends.

I pictured my father's longing gaze as he stood soaking wet on the marina's dock, watching me drift out to sea. He had no way of knowing when I'd make it back—if I ever did. I thought of the sea stone and everything the Sea Haven Council had taken from us all, and I worried about what the council might be doing to my friends and family back home.

I became furious, until all that rage rose to the surface and culminated in a potent connection with the sea. I could feel it oscillating through me, igniting every nerve within my body until I was trembling with power unlike any I'd ever felt before. Internally, I pleaded with the sea for a release, until her brewing storm beneath the surface matched the rhythm of my own.

I tugged on that power deep within the sea again, and when I did, water rose up around me. The energy retreated, and this time, I didn't hang on to it. I let it fall away like a wave.

Then the energy swung back in my direction, slightly stronger this time. I began to *feel* the dance Tristan had described. I did this again, allowing the power of the sea to pull away from me, before yanking it back in my direction. Each time the energy retreated further away from me, it only came back stronger.

"You're doing it," Tristan encouraged.

Overhead, clouds had started to roll in, blocking out the bright sun. Pride washed through me as I saw it was working. I climbed onto a rock that jutted out of the water, moving my arms with the rhythm of the ocean's power. Her energy filled me up, then retreated again, and I started to *dance*, swaying forward on one foot to the rhythm of the waves, before leaning back to pull my magic in, filling me with power from head to toe.

Darkness swelled overhead, and lightning flashed in the distance. My face grew hot as I kept the momentum building.

Tristan transformed into his legs to come stand beside me. "Keep going! You're doing great."

I moved faster, twisting and spinning as I played a game with the ocean and brought her storm to me. Waves began to crash upon the ocean's surface, and thunder cracked loudly overhead. The wind picked up and sent my hair flying around my face, but I kept on going. The immense power of the sea grew, and once we were in sync, I commanded huge ocean waves to rise up and collide, causing white water to spray for miles.

A rage-filled scream broke from my chest as I unleashed my fury upon the ocean's surface. My voice echoed to the sky and back. Overhead, the clouds let free a torrential downpour. Heavy rain pounded down on us, pelting against the rock. It didn't bother me in the slightest. If anything, the rainwater filled me with a renewed sense of vitality.

Immense relief flooded through me, and my scream turned to laughter as I fell to my knees. I hadn't expected it to feel this *good*.

"You did it!" Tristan cried. "Now, work with the sea to calm the storm. Just as you brought this energy to you, you can work with it to transform it and cause the storm to retreat."

I feared I might lose control, the way I always did when things became too much and my anger exploded out of me. But I was surprised to find that expressing myself in this way felt wholly freeing, giving me *more* control over the storm overhead. I didn't have to hold it back, only let my clouds run out of rain.

It didn't take long for the rainstorm to calm to a slow drizzle. I did as Tristan instructed, moving and swaying to the pulsing power of the sea. As power swelled upward, I welcomed it instead of resisting it, until my magic was working in partnership with the sea. I drew a deep breath to calm myself, and the ocean responded to match my energy.

Another wave of magic rose upward, but not quite as strong this time. I kept the rhythm going, until the thunder reduced to a low rumble and the clouds began to recede. The ocean's surface settled, and the storm dissolved overhead.

"That was excellent," Tristan said. "How did you achieve that so easily?"

"I just tapped into the torrent already inside of me, and I felt what the sea feels," I explained. "I've always been told I'm too bold or rash, but maybe that's not a bad thing. If I channel these aspects of myself correctly, I could use them to help people, to brew a storm big enough to defeat the council!"

Tristan raised an eyebrow, appearing impressed. "If you can do that, we should have your siren call and tail in no time."

I sat upon the rock, exhausted by the power I'd wielded. Sunlight shone down on us, warming my skin. "I didn't know I was capable of that. I would've expected conjuring a storm to be the most difficult magic to access. I wonder why I can do that, but my other powers seem blocked."

Tristan sat beside me and ran his fingers through his beard curiously. "I've been thinking. In the Luna Pod, young merfolk learning their sonic scream can experience difficulty using it until they find and connect with the voice within themselves. Then there are other times, like you saw with Ronan's mother at the memorial, when a merfolk's voice is silenced when they're unable to express themselves. Perhaps this phenomenon with your tail and siren call is similar."

"Do you think that's why I was able to use my sonic scream against Carson Ray?" I wondered. "Because I spoke up for myself and refused to be silenced?"

"That would make sense, which makes me wonder if your inability to summon your tail or siren call *is* a lasting effect of the sea stone, but not in the magical sense," Tristan mused. "Perhaps by being disconnected from your magic all this time, you aren't sure how to express it. This storm was easy for you because you're already used to the storm inside of you, and now you have to learn how to connect with other aspects of your magic."

I contemplated his words for a few moments, letting them sink in. "That sounds right. What do I need in order to express this power?"

Tristan thought about it. "I can't say for sure. People on shore think siren songs are a bad omen, but to us they're a sign of hope, because we use it for protection."

"So maybe... I'm afraid to protect myself," I suggested.

"Perhaps." Tristan placed his hand atop mine on the rock. "If that's the case, then there's hope. All we need to do is practice connecting to those pieces of yourself, and you will find the magic within you."

I squeezed his hand back, and my stomach fluttered like there was a school of a hundred tiny fish swimming around inside of it. "Thank you for your help. I may not have all my merfolk powers yet, but summoning a storm proves that I'm more than Sea Haven ever wanted me to be."

Tristan smiled. "But you still can't outswim me."

I nudged my shoulder against his. "Is that right, fish boy?"

Tristan laughed and got to his feet. "If you want to swim faster, I have an idea. Follow me."

CHAPTER 10

Tristan and I returned to Luna City, where he led me through winding twists and turns in the rock that appeared like roadways leading past underwater shops and restaurants. He slowed as we came upon a wide opening, which had a sign out front decorated in seashells that read *The Marina*.

"This must be Cordelia's shop," I said.

"It is," Tristan replied. "Come on in. You'll love it."

Tristan led me inside a large cavern that was anything but cave-like. Though the shop was housed within the rock, it was more grand and elaborate than any architecture back home. The tall ceiling was carved with intricate archways, and a seashell chandelier hung beneath a hole overhead that caused sunlight to shimmer off every surface.

Along the walls were displays of beautiful weapons, from colorful spears to elaborate tridents. We swam past a display of daggers that were carved from some sort of rock that looked like ice, and an entire wall was dedicated to beautiful shields and matching armor. Another display was filled with seashell handbags, gorgeous necklaces, and hand-crafted tiaras. Anything and everything that could be carved or handmade was here, and it was all incredible and breathtaking.

Tristan led me to the back of the store, where I heard a familiar voice. We rounded a display and came upon Noah and Cordelia at a countertop, hovering over a silver spear with a dark blue stone set into it. Noah's mentor Lamar was nearby, admiring a green shield.

"This spear is longer than the last one we looked at, and the tip is heavier, but I think it will suit you well," Cordelia was saying.

Noah lifted the spear and tested its center of gravity, spinning it around a few times. "I like it. This one feels more natural than the last one—"

Noah lifted his gaze and cut off when he saw us. His eyes lit up. "Bree, come look. What do you think?"

I swam over and observed the spear. It was so beautiful that I couldn't imagine doing any harm with it. The dark blue stone even matched his cerulean scales. "I love it. If it feels good to you, then you should get it."

"It does suit you," Cordelia agreed.

Noah smiled. "I'll get this one then."

He handed it back, and Cordelia placed it back on the counter. "I'll get it engraved with your name and delivered to your quarters tomorrow, then."

"Sounds good," Noah said.

"What do you think of this shield?" Lamar asked, holding up a silver metal plate with blue edging.

Noah swam over to look at shields with Lamar.

Cordelia turned to us. "What can I help you two with?"

Tristan leaned against the counter. "I had an idea that might help Bree swim faster. Do you have any fins available?"

Cordelia frowned. "I do, but they aren't designed for legs."

"I was thinking we could modify them," Tristan said.

"What do you mean?" I asked.

Cordelia sighed. "Wait here."

She swam through a doorway behind the counter, then returned a few moments later with what looked like a synthetic mermaid tail draped over her arms. The fins were light blue, with a clear sleeve that looked like it could be slipped over the end of a mermaid's tail.

Cordelia caught me eyeing the fins. "I designed these prosthetics for merfolk who have lost their fins due to shark attacks, infection, or other accidents," she explained. "The sleeve is designed for a merfolk's tail, though. It won't fit over your legs securely, and even if it did, the fins wouldn't move right because legs don't bend the same way a tail does. It could help with speed, but you won't have the same precision and maneuverability, so it really depends on what you're looking for."

"What if instead of trying to replace my legs with a tail, we work *with* my anatomy?" I wondered.

Tristan ran his fingers through his beard. "I see what you're saying. Could we cut the fins in half and fit them to her feet to give more power to her kicks?"

"We can, but it will take a few days to modify it," Cordelia said.

"I can wait," I offered. "I think I'd rather have precision over speed to start out with."

Cordelia nodded. "All right. I'll need to measure your feet to get them fitted properly."

"That's really kind of you," I said. "This would really help me move through the water better."

Cordelia cocked her head. "Come to the back with me, and I'll take your measurements."

"This is where I'll leave you," Tristan told me. "Our training is finished for today, and we will pick back up tomorrow. You made great progress."

"Thanks," I said. "It was a lot of fun."

I waved goodbye and followed Cordelia into the back. We entered a small room that looked like a dressing room, with multiple prosthetic fins dangling from racks. On the wall hung long skirts that looked to be crafted out of a silky seaweed fabric, with matching tops that I figured mermaids wore when they went on land.

"Have a seat," Cordelia said, though she barely glanced

at me. I could swear the water dropped several degrees once we were alone.

I sat along a bench that had been carved from the rock. Cordelia positioned herself below me and held up the blue fins to my feet, assessing the sizing. I watched her curiously as she moved the fins one way, then the other, then flipped them over like she was trying to visualize how this was going to work.

She didn't say anything, but I could feel the tension in the air. It was obvious since I arrived that Cordelia didn't like me. She seemed reluctant to help me, almost like she had no choice because the prince requested it. The silence was really awkward.

"You and Tristan seem to be getting along well," Cordelia said, cutting through the quiet.

I nodded. "Yeah, he's been really helpful so far."

"He mentioned you were making progress," she added shortly, which made her really hard to read.

"I summoned a storm today, but I still don't have my siren call or my tail," I replied.

Cordelia started marking a few spots on the fins with pins. "You and Tristan sound like you're enjoying your time together. Do you like him?"

I wasn't sure what she was getting at, so I chose my words carefully. "Tristan is a great guy, but we hardly know each other. He's just teaching me some things about my magic I never learned back home."

She cocked an eyebrow. "So he's *just* your mentor?"

Now I could sense the aggression in her tone, and I bit back sharply, "Yes, just my mentor."

"*Right...*" Cordelia didn't sound convinced. "I saw the way you looked at him at breakfast."

She was clearly trying to accuse me of something, and I wasn't interested in playing games with her.

"If you have something to say, just say it," I bit harshly. "It's obvious you disliked me from the moment I arrived. At first I thought it was about where I came from, but you've been nice to Liana and Noah, so I can only assume this is about something else entirely. It's about Tristan, isn't it? If you think I'm going to hurt him, you don't have to worry about that."

Cordelia gave an amused laugh. "Tristan didn't tell you, did he? I knew it. I could see it the moment you swam into the throne room, clinging to his back like some little barnacle."

I reeled back, yanking my foot away from her. "Go ahead, Cordelia. Tell me what you *really* think."

She swished her fins through the water, until she'd risen to her full height to loom above me. "I think you have no idea who you're dealing with. Don't think I didn't notice you two sneaking off together after the memorial. You and Tristan have been spending a lot of time alone together lately, and I hardly think that's appropriate for a betrothed man."

"Betrothed?" I repeated, grasping at the word. I couldn't have heard her right.

"Who exactly did you think I was?" she demanded

cruelly. "I'm not just some pretty face swimming leisurely around the palace. I'm next in line to be queen—better known as Tristan's *fiancé*."

My heart gave a stuttered jolt, but I swallowed down the shock. Tristan had certainly never mentioned being *engaged*... though, why should he? It wasn't like I had any claim over him.

"You can calm your fins," I told her. "There's nothing going on between Tristan and me, and I would never try to get between you two."

I wondered, then, why a small part of me felt shattered by her admission.

Cordelia sank slightly in the water, looking pleased. "Of course there's nothing going on between you two. It doesn't change the fact that Tristan didn't tell you about us, and don't you try to deny it. I saw that look written all over your face."

I narrowed my eyes. "If you're jealous, then that sounds like a problem between you and him. I don't know why Tristan didn't say anything to me, but maybe because it's none of my business. If you don't trust him to spend time with another girl, then maybe you two shouldn't be getting married."

It was cruel what I'd said to her. I realized it the second it came out of my mouth, but I couldn't take it back.

Cordelia inched back, pursing her lips. "You're right. It *is* none of your business."

I glanced down to the fins she'd set aside. "If you dislike me that much, why are you helping me?"

She scoffed. "I don't have to like you to help you. You're a mermaid in Luna City, which means you're part of this community, and in *my* pod we help each other."

Cordelia didn't hesitate to emphasize the *my pod* part.

"Though, if you want to blend in, you should probably start with covering up those legs of yours." She gestured to the skirts on the wall. "These should do the trick. Take your pick."

As if I wanted to take anything more from her. I already owed her for the fins. "I'm fine, thanks."

"Well, if you change your mind, you know where to find them." She snatched up the fins and turned away. "I'll have these fins modified and back to you next week. In the meantime, I believe we're both on the same page."

In other words, *keep your hands off my man.*

"Absolutely," I replied coldly, rising from the bench. "You have nothing to worry about."

I kicked off the ground and swam out of the room as fast as I could, reeling from the entire conversation. I was really confused about all of it. Tristan and I had been getting along, but we hadn't been *flirting*... or had we? He'd taken my hand in his more than once, and we'd been teasing each other all morning. Was that what Cordelia was worried about, or was Tristan just being kind?

I wasn't sure how to feel, but at the core of it, I was most confused why Tristan didn't tell me. It'd have been easy to slip into our introductions. *"This is Cordelia, by the way, my betrothed."* Or he could've brought it up literally any other time we'd been together.

It all felt weird. If I was engaged, I'd want everyone to know how in love I was. But Tristan and Cordelia? They didn't make sense together. He barely glanced her way in her presence, and she seemed strangely possessive of him.

But he wasn't mine to worry about... nor mine to *want*. Whatever was going on was between the two of *them*, and Cordelia had made it clear that the best thing I could do was stay out of her way. I was here in Luna City to grow my powers, help the pod, and eventually restore magic to Sea Haven. My duty was to my own pod, and I didn't need feelings for a guy I'd only just met getting in the way of that—

My thoughts skidded to a halt when I left the shop and nearly ran into someone. I kicked backward and looked up to see Noah waiting there. My racing heart slowed.

"Hey, I heard you're getting fins," he said brightly.

"Yeah, Cordelia is going to work on them this week."

I must've still been shaken up from the conversation, because Noah's features fell. "Is something wrong?"

I shook my head. It seemed awkward to mention my encounter with Cordelia to him. "I'm fine. Just... missing home, I guess."

Noah offered a kind smile. "In that case, I know something that might cheer you up."

CHAPTER 11

Noah and I swam high above the rock formations and past the palace, until we came upon an open expanse of white sand. Merfolk of all ages filled the area and were building underwater sandcastles or tossing balls made of seaweed back and forth. Young children swam races, and others danced with fish and other marine animals nearby while adults sang a beautiful, upbeat melody. At the edge of the sand, various vendors were selling food and handmade art. It reminded me of the beach back home.

"Lamar showed me this place earlier," Noah said. "They call it the Bar."

"Ah, like a sand bar," I noted. "A bit different from what a bar means back home."

Noah laughed. "Come on. There's an open spot over here."

We swam downward to a secluded area. Noah sat in the sand, unfurling his fins across the ocean floor as he began tracing lines through it. "I remember one year at the Sea Festival, we competed in the sandcastle building competition. You took home first place with a sculpture of coral."

I tilted my head to the side and sat beside him. "I can't believe you remember that. I couldn't have been more than ten at the time."

Noah smirked. "I could never forget the girl who beat me to the trophy," he teased. "I came in second."

"Really?" I began to gather sand around me, drawing it into a pile. "I don't remember that. What'd you sculpt?"

"I made a replica of the old lighthouse."

"Wait, I *do* remember that!" I recalled. "It was really good, too. But then..."

"The seagull," Noah laughed. "He landed on top of my lighthouse and ruined it. I didn't have the time to fix it."

I shook my head. "That darn seagull. Tell you what, I'll challenge you to a rematch."

Noah cocked an eyebrow. "Think you can beat me again?"

I crinkled my nose. "I'll give it my best shot."

Noah and I got to work on our sand sculptures, though Cordelia's threats still echoed in the back of my head. I began by packing sand together in a heap, then started carving a face and tentacles to make an octopus. I peered over at Noah's sculpture to see that he was replicating our town's lighthouse. It was really intricate and detailed. I had no idea he was so talented.

"Done," he finally announced.

"Me, too." I stepped back to admire our sand art, and Noah swam higher to get a good look at it.

"Impressive," he said approvingly. "This octopus almost looks real."

I placed my hands on my hips. "Is it better than your lighthouse, though? Because it looks to me like Noah Starr could give me a run for my money."

His sculpture stood as high as my knee and looked like a perfect replica of our lighthouse. He'd even carved out the rocks at the base and added windows at the top.

"Mama!" a young child cried. Three kids, all sharing the same aquamarine scales, swam by with their mother. The youngest tugged on her mom's hand, swishing her tail back and forth insistently. "Look at the octopus!"

The mother offered a kind smile. "Hi, I'm Naia, and these are Maisie, Beck, and Pearl. Do you mind if we take a look?"

"Not at all," I said, before turning to the children. "We actually need some judges to decide which sculpture is better. Would you three want to vote for the winner?"

Naia smiled. "Oh, I don't think this is fair. My daughters *love* octopuses."

The oldest girl, Maisie, who couldn't be more than

eight years old, swam around the octopus to observe it. "I want to pick him up and hug him!"

"I think the lighthouse is cool!" the young boy, Beck, said.

"Then it looks like we need a tie breaker," I told them. "What do you think, Pearl?"

The smallest mergirl looked around three years old. She swam toward us, but instead of going for the sand sculptures, she stopped at my feet and reached out to touch my toes.

"Your fins look funny!" Pearl said with a laugh.

I was momentarily stunned, not sure what to say to the little girl.

Naia gasped. "I'm so sorry!"

I shifted uncomfortably, but said, "It's okay. We all have feet, right?"

I wiggled my toes at Pearl, digging them into the sand a little. The other two kids lit up as they came to surround their sister and took turns poking at and tickling my toes.

Maisie crinkled her nose. "I went on land on my birthday to summon my legs, and I fell over."

Naia sighed. "She walks just fine. She just stepped on a rock."

"It hurt!" Maisie cried, before turning back to me. "Is swimming hard with feet?"

"I'm slow over long distances," I admitted. "But I'm a strong swimmer."

"Can you dance?" Beck asked.

I nodded. "Oh, yes, I dance all the time."

"Can we see!?" Pearl exclaimed.

Maisie's eyes lit up, and she pointed to a group of children nearby spinning to their parents' song. "They won't care if we join them!"

I hesitated, but I figured it couldn't hurt anything. "Um... sure, why not?"

I gestured for the kids to follow me, and we swam over to the group of merfolk playing music. "Can we join in?"

An older woman waved us forward. "Of course! Come on in."

I stepped into the group of dancers and sea creatures that were swirling around in circles. Around us, merfolk beat rocks together and blew through conch shells to make all kinds of music, while the older woman's voice swelled above it all in another language that sounded like an old folk tune.

I planted my feet in the sand and spun in circles, showing the children how I jumped and leapt to dance on my feet. Their eyes sparkled with intrigue as they joined hands and began swimming circles around me. Fish rushed to join in, until I was encased in a cyclone of color, dancing with everything from clownfish and parrotfish to squid, rays, and crabs.

The beat picked up, and we spun faster and faster until our laughter was ringing all across the Bar. Noah watched from afar, wearing a wide smile.

As my eyes locked on him, Pearl took notice. She swam over and grabbed his hand, yanking him toward our circle. "Come dance!" she cried.

"All right, if you insist," Noah replied playfully. He cut through the fish swirling around us and joined me in the center of the circle.

We grabbed hands and spun faster, my heart speeding up to the beat of the music. Noah swished his tail, increasing his speed until my feet lifted off the sand and we spiraled higher in the water. The fish followed to continue the dance.

My fingers began to slip out of his, but I couldn't help laughing. "Don't let go!"

Noah yanked me closer, securing his arms around me as his tail sent us spinning so fast that the ocean around us became a blur. "Never."

That racing feeling in my chest calmed, even as we twirled in circles. The singing and cheers from below us seemed to fade. In Noah's arms, my mind quieted, and I could effortlessly forget about my less-than-friendly chat with Cordelia. This hug didn't feel awkward; it felt entirely natural. I'd been confused about Tristan earlier, but with Noah everything felt clear, and I was completely safe in his presence.

The song built to a crescendo, and the two of us fell into the sand beside the children, laughing because we'd gotten so dizzy the ocean seemed to be swirling around us. I fell on top of Noah, and he cradled me to his chest.

The sounds around us came rushing back as cheers rang out across the sandbar and the song faded to an end. I glanced up to see over a dozen merfolk had gathered around, their curious eyes on me. I really did look out of place, swimming through their city with my legs and odd clothing.

I folded my legs closer to me, and their gazes darted away from me when they saw that I'd noticed them staring.

Pearl popped up from the sand, her dizziness forgotten. "Let's do that again!"

"I think that's enough spinning for me today," I teased. "But thank you for inviting me to dance."

Pearl and her family waved goodbye. "Come back again!"

Noah and I swam away as another song started up again and the children got lost in the dance. I was glad to get away from the strange looks I kept getting.

To distract myself, I said, "We never determined who won the sand sculpture contest."

"Let's call it a tie," he suggested.

"Deal," I agreed. Then, without thinking about it, I threw my arms around Noah and pulled him into a hug. He stiffened for a moment, before relaxing into it and drawing me closer. "Thank you for bringing me here. The lighthouse you made really does remind me of home."

"Yeah, it was no problem," Noah said, before releasing me.

As I drew away, I heard someone calling my name. I turned around to see Liana swimming toward me, her golden scales shimmering in the afternoon sun. "Bree, Noah! Maren said I might find you here. How was everyone's training sessions?"

"Mine was good," Noah said. "I got a tour of the

academy and started training in evacuation protocols. Afterward, I got to pick out a spear. Did you know they don't have money in Luna City? They trade and barter things instead."

"What'd you trade for your spear?" Liana asked.

"Stories," Noah said. "We didn't exactly come here with much. That's all I've got."

Liana smiled. "That's so beautiful that the Luna pod accepts stories as currency. Everyone has a story to tell."

"Speaking of currency, I'm going to trade something for some fish at one of the food vendors," Noah announced. "Would you two like anything?"

"Sure, I'm pretty hungry," Liana said.

"Me, too," I agreed.

Liana held her breath as Noah swam off, before he was finally out of earshot. "You won't believe what happened to me this morning! After breakfast, I ran into Zale in the hall, and he wanted to talk more about the surface, so I swam with him to the edge of the city. On the way, he took me to this underwater library. We talked forever, until Maren finally found me and Zale had to go back to the rig. Anyway, the prince wants me to record some of my stories and add them to the records!"

"That sounds amazing, and *way* more interesting than what happened to me."

Liana raised her eyebrows and gasped dramatically. "Do I sense some *boy* drama?"

"What, no?" I shot a glance over at Noah, who was

waiting in line at one of the food booths. My cheeks heated.

"Liar," Liana accused.

"Let's go sit down," I suggested.

Liana and I found our way to a rock formation at the edge of the sand, where we both took a seat and leaned together to speak in low whispers.

"I want to know *everything*," she gushed.

"Tristan is *engaged*. To Cordelia," I told her.

Liana gasped. "No way. I knew something was going on with that girl. The way she looked at you during breakfast was hostile."

"So was the conversation we had at The Marina earlier," I said, before diving into an explanation.

Liana leaned back on her rock when I finished. "What is this girl's problem? It's not like you're going to come in and steal the Luna pod from her."

I shook my head. "She thinks I'm going to steal her man."

Liana cocked an eyebrow. "Well, are you? I've seen the way you look at Tristan."

"That was before I knew he was engaged," I said. "I'm not going to get in the middle of someone else's relationship. There are plenty of other men in the sea."

"Literally," Liana chuckled.

I shot another glance at Noah, who was still waiting for his fish.

Liana followed my gaze. "I knew it! You have feelings for Noah, don't you?"

I scoffed. "No, it's just... Noah saved me and gave up his life to get my magic back. I owe him everything."

"*Everything?*" Liana wiggled her eyebrows.

I shoved her lightly in the shoulder. "Not like that! Maybe... I don't know."

Liana eyed me up and down, teasing, "Bree Waters has gone speechless, and for a man, no less. Or is it *two* men?"

I felt my cheeks heat again. "I'm not even thinking about guys like that, Liana. Even if I liked Tristan— which I *don't*— he's taken. And Noah is—"

"Available?" she cut in.

I frowned. "Noah's *a friend*."

"A friend who stays the night?" she joked.

"He did *not* stay the night with me," I insisted. "He swam me back to the boat, and we just *talked*."

"You did *something* with your mouths, I'm sure."

I rolled my eyes. Noah and I hadn't kissed, and I didn't know what possessed Liana to think that we *would*.

"If it were me, I wouldn't waste my time on a man who's already taken," Liana insisted. "Especially not when there's a hottie already waiting for you."

"Noah is not *waiting* for me."

Liana shrugged. "You never know unless you ask."

I tried to picture myself with Noah, and I could see it... but not without images of Tristan's hand on mine invading my thoughts.

"Maybe I am torn between them," I admitted. "Tristan makes me feel like there are schools of fish swimming around in my belly, while Noah's like a warm blanket that keeps me warm. But it's not like anything could ever happen between Tristan and me. I just wish I'd heard about his engagement from him first, instead of pissing off Cordelia. I don't know why he didn't bring it up, or if I should ask him about it."

"There's no need to stir the pot," Liana said.

I eyed her sideways and teased, "But that's what I do best."

"You know what happens when you open your big mouth. It's best to try not to feel anything for Tristan and just treat him as a mentor. In the meantime, it can't hurt to explore this thing with Noah."

Liana was right.

So why did it feel like choosing between them might ruin me?

CHAPTER 12

I tried to take Liana's advice, but my feelings only became more complex as I spent my days exploring Luna City with Tristan and my nights deep in conversation with Noah. I used to go on late-night walks on the beach when I couldn't sleep; now I stayed up talking with Noah. Each night, he stayed on the boat longer than the last as we shared stories from back home, admitted secrets we'd never told anyone else, and confided our deepest fears in one another. I felt like I could tell him anything.

Except for one thing. No matter how much I opened up to Noah, I still couldn't admit how I felt about him.

We'd been connecting on such a deep level, and I feared that telling him I was developing feelings for him could ruin what we had, or shift focus from what we were truly here to do.

Then there was Tristan. We'd continued our training, and while I'd felt a new tension in the air after Cordelia's admission, Tristan didn't seem to pick up on it. I'd waited for him to bring up his engagement, but he never mentioned it. It bothered me, because it felt like we were both hiding something behind our kind smiles and silly jokes, though I couldn't be sure what he was thinking. It was driving me nuts.

A week and a half passed before Cordelia finished with my fins. Tristan presented them to me when he met me in the lagoon one morning.

"What do you think?" he asked, holding the fins above the surface of the water. Tristan appeared wholly nonchalant, as he had every day for the past week. He still wasn't aware that I knew about the engagement.

I crossed the deck to the railing, my skirt swaying around my legs. After that day at the Bar, I decided Cordelia was right and a skirt would help keep people from staring. I didn't *want* to ask for her help again, but I needed extra clothes anyway. The skirt I wore today was made out of blue seaweed and had various slits up to my hips that gave me a wide range of motion, even in the water. It came with a matching seashell bra that fit perfectly.

I peered over the edge of the boat, smiling when my

gaze met Tristan's blue-green eyes. I couldn't help it. Despite the unspoken words between us, being around Tristan always brightened my mood.

I eyed the fins he was holding. Cordelia had modified them to look like scuba fins, with footholds for my feet. The fins themselves were long and webbed, and they shimmered a beautiful sky blue to match my skirt.

"I love them," I told him.

"Sit," Tristan instructed. "I'll help you into them."

I situated myself at the edge of the deck, dangling my feet toward the water. Tristan reached for my foot, and tingles spread up my leg. I tried to ignore the feeling, but that electric sizzle I felt every time we touched had only intensified since arriving in Luna City. It didn't help that I clung to Tristan's back everywhere we went, though with these new fins I'd finally be able to keep up on my own. Maybe then these strange feelings I had for him would go away.

"How do they feel?" Tristan asked once he slipped both fins on.

I kicked my feet, splashing a few droplets of water in his face. He cocked a stern eyebrow, and I laughed, which helped curb the unease in my gut. When I was laughing with Tristan, it felt like we had no care in the world.

"The fins feel secure," I said. "Let's see what they feel like in the water."

I slid underneath the deck railing and jumped into the lagoon, inhaling a deep breath of saltwater. I kicked my feet, and the fins sliced through the water to propel me forward. Using my powers, I commanded the ocean to move like a current around me, rocketing me forward. My heart seemed to drop from my chest as I reached the other side of the lagoon in seconds. It felt exhilarating and frightening all at the same time.

I slowed to catch my breath and spun toward Tristan, who had followed and was only a few feet behind me. A grin spread across my face. "These fins are amazing."

"How are they working with the skirt?" he asked. "Is it slowing you down at all?"

I spun through the water. "No, the skirt's great."

Tristan frowned. "I don't want you to feel like you have to cover up. Your legs are part of who you are."

I shrugged. "I don't want everyone looking at me like I'm different."

"You're still a merfolk," he insisted. "You're just at a different spot on your journey."

I liked that Tristan didn't treat me like there was something wrong with me, but I still wasn't taking off the skirt. "I like the skirt. It makes me feel fancy."

"Fair enough." Tristan cocked his head. "Come on. We'll swim at your pace today. I want you to get a feel for swimming with fins, and I'm hoping that will help us ease into summoning your tail."

"All right, where are we swimming to?"

Tristan smiled. "I know just the place."

He led me out of the lagoon and into deeper waters. I was surprised by how effortlessly I seemed to move through the ocean. I closed my eyes, trying to picture these fins as an extension of myself like it'd be if I could summon my mermaid tail.

"What do you think?" Tristan asked.

"I feel like I've been swimming with a weight around my chest my whole life and now out here in the open waters, I'm light and free," I admitted. "It's hard to imagine what it will be like with a tail, because I've never truly experienced it before."

"Just keep feeling into it," Tristan encouraged. "It's just a matter of getting used to it."

I kept my eyes closed and began to twist and spin through the water in a way that felt natural to me. I darted one way, then the other, using the fins to create sharp turns and to spiral effortlessly as I changed direction.

"There you go!" Tristan cheered.

I opened my eyes to see that he was following beside me, swirling through the water as if we were dancing with the ocean itself. I smiled as I darted downward, swimming in an arc around him.

Tristan laughed. "Now *you're* swimming circles around *me*. You'll have your tail in no time."

"I hope so," I said. "This feels so natural."

"It should," he replied. "It's in your blood, Bree. We'll find your tail. I know it."

We kept on swimming, darting around tall rock formations and twisting through schools of fish as we passed. I felt so invigorated, so alive.

We must've been swimming for miles, because I had

no idea where we were anymore. We were far away from the city, and I didn't recognize any of the rocks or coral.

"Where are you taking me?" I asked.

Tristan pointed ahead. The water was deep and murkier than it was in the city, so it was hard to make out what he was looking at. "It's not much further. It's just up there."

I followed Tristan, though he swam slower so that I could keep up. I kept my eyes on where he'd pointed, toward a cluster of rocks piled upon the ocean floor. Only when we came closer did the rocks become more clear, and I realized the formation I'd been watching wasn't made entirely of rocks at all. In the middle of it all were boards and beams, and a tall mast covered in seaweed.

It was a shipwreck.

CHAPTER 13

My gaze darted from one end of the ship to the other as we approached. It looked to be an old ship that must've crashed here over a hundred years ago. I had no doubt that the Luna pod took it down themselves to protect their city. The ship was slowly being consumed by the sea, as it was completely covered in a thick layer of algae. The sunlight barely reached us here, though the darkness didn't bother me. It felt quiet and peaceful being this far from the surface.

"What is this place?" I asked.

"It's one of the few remaining shipwrecks in the area,"

Tristan explained. "Seafolk rarely come here because it's outside the enchantment of the island, but who's going to question the prince?"

He gave a playful wink, which caused my breath to catch.

"So we really shouldn't be here?" I asked.

Tristan shrugged as we approached the shipwreck. "It's no big deal. I used to come here all the time with my brother when we were kids. Our mother pretended not to know about it, but somehow the guards *always* found us when she wanted us back home."

It was the first time I'd ever heard Tristan mention his mother. I'd noticed the queen was never around, but no one had ever brought her up before now. I still didn't know what had happened to her.

"That's kind of sweet that she let you two have your fun," I said.

"She wanted us to feel normal—as normal as we could being royals. Here at the shipwreck, outside the confines of the palace, Zale and I could just be normal kids."

Tristan led me to a huge hole in the side of the ship wall. We entered through the hull, where the water was calm and a dark blue hue filled the space.

Inside the cabin, there was so much to explore—tables that still stood upright, paintings on the walls that were barely discernable past the barnacles growing on them, and various sizes of pottery that lined a ledge. Leaning up against the center of the nearest wall was a huge anchor, which had far less growth on it than the rest of the ship.

Tristan followed my gaze and stopped beside the anchor to run his hands over the metal. "This anchor is original to this ship. Zale and I dragged it in here and cleaned it up a few years ago, once we were strong enough to move it. We always wanted to preserve the items we found from the surface, so this shipwreck sort of became a secret gallery for our collection."

My fingers trailed over the top of an old chest. "What's this, then? A treasure chest?"

Tristan laughed. "Funny you should say that, because that's exactly what we used to call it. Go ahead, you can open it."

I opened the top and found all sorts of trinkets inside, from a hand-held mirror to old maps and several pieces of jewelry that still shimmered in the dim lighting. I lifted one of the necklaces, which had a large blue emerald-cut stone surrounded by clear gems.

"Huh," Tristan mused as he came up behind me. "I didn't know this was here."

I handed him the necklace. "Is it valuable? It looks like aquamarine."

"It is," Tristan said. "In the Luna pod, aquamarine is a stone for royals, though it's more sentimental than valuable."

I remembered Tristan saying aquamarine was the stone of his people, and they believed it provided protection. In reality, it shielded the wearer from the effects of the Sea Haven Council's sea stone. I still had the aquamarine necklace I'd taken from Carson, tucked in a drawer back on the boat, but I wanted nothing to do with anything that once belonged to him. This necklace was far more beautiful and clearly made to draw the eye.

Tristan ran his thumb over the blue gem. "This was my mother's. She got it on an expedition to the surface that she went on when she was around my age. I knew Zale kept it after she passed, but I assumed it was still in his quarters at the palace. This necklace came from the surface, though, so he must've brought it here to add to our collection. I didn't know he was still collecting things."

"You haven't been here in a while, then?" I wondered.

Tristan shook his head. "This was just a childhood pastime. Once we were older and tasked with more responsibilities, we rarely came here. Zale must've come back to place this here in our mother's honor."

Tristan got a look of fondness in his eyes when he spoke of his mother.

"Did your mother go on a lot of expeditions?" I asked.

"No, just the one, though she spoke of it often, turning her experience into bedtime stories," Tristan said. "My brother and I became fascinated with the surface, so this shipwreck was really special to us. We used to come out here and pretend we were sailors."

I chuckled. "It's funny that you would pretend you were human, when back home all we played was mermaids."

Tristan gave a hesitant smile as he placed the necklace back in the chest. "I wish the real thing was as magical as it felt when we were playing make-believe."

My heart sank, and I wasn't sure I should ask, but it seemed Tristan was awaiting the question. "You're referring to your mom?"

He averted his gaze. "Yes, my mother, Queen Lorelei, died last year shortly after the Ocean Rock drillship arrived."

I thought back to that first day at breakfast and how Lamar had mentioned a massacre. I hadn't realized he'd been speaking of recent events. "What happened, exactly?"

Tristan turned from me and swam over to a window, leaning his elbows on the edge to peer out into the expanse of ocean before us. "A year ago, Ocean Rock arrived with a drillship and began mining oil nearby. We knew drillships are temporary vessels typically used for exploring and locating resources, so we left them alone at first, because we couldn't risk exposing ourselves. We hoped they'd find nothing and leave on their own. But then one of their hoses ruptured while transporting oil to a shuttle tanker. That was the first incident that caused damage to our ecosystem."

"The first?" I asked.

Tristan nodded. "We used siren compulsion to drive that first drillship away. They capped their well and left, so we thought we were free of them. Then they came back, with a bigger ship and more resources, and they began drilling again. Things got worse, and the reefs surrounding our cities started dying off. We knew then that siren compulsion wasn't enough, because they'd only send others."

Tristan inhaled deeply. "This time, we tried to drive them out by force, hoping that rough seas or the threat of dangerous sea creatures would scare them off for good. But we weren't prepared for the technological advances they had aboard. Harpoons and nets like we'd seen in the past were only the beginning. Now they had all this technology to track us through the water, and their harpoon cannons had explosives attached. They keep these weapons aboard in case of animal attacks, and we were one hell of an animal."

"I thought your existence was still a secret," I remarked. "Were your people exposed that day?"

Tristan shook his head. "We attacked, but they weren't able to identify *what* was attacking them, so our identity remains concealed. But things didn't go as planned. In our pod, it's the queen's job to make decisions, and the king's role to give the orders and delegate tasks. It's imperative that they work together, and that day, my parents were divided. My mother saw that we didn't stand a chance and made the decision to retreat, but my father thought we could defeat them, so he hesitated to give the order. That moment of division cost us dearly."

He dropped his head. "We lost a lot of people, including the queen. What's more, our attack damaged one of their pipes, and the oil leak contaminated our waters further. Driving these people out by force can't work, because there's a process to safely disconnect the equipment, and using force risks further damage."

Tristan sighed. "We withdrew and did our best to recuperate from the losses, but our ecosystem kept on dying."

"And no one blames the king for what happened?" I wondered.

"It all happened so fast. I don't think it's right to blame him, though I worry for the future because he hasn't been the same since my mother died. My father gives the orders, but my mother moved the people. Without a queen, my dad doesn't know what to do, because the queen makes the decisions, from expanding the city to determining when to go to war. The monarchy runs best when run by partners who support one another. Regardless, my mother's no longer here, and we still need that fierce king my father once was to lead us through this."

"If your father can no longer manage alone, why doesn't he pass on the crown to you?" I asked.

Tristan drew a deep breath. "He would, if he thought I was ready."

I noticed hesitation in his tone. "Don't you want to be king?"

"I do. All I want is to do right by my people, but I'd want to do it in my own way, and my father wishes for me to follow tradition," Tristan said. "My father is pushing me to become king, but he also won't give up the crown until this is all over. He doesn't wish to alarm our people with a change in leadership right now, but what he fails to realize is that we're running out of time. After the massacre,

Ocean Rock showed up with the equipment to install a permanent rig, which they're piecing together as we speak. Once that drill hits the ocean floor, it's over. A permanent operation will destroy our ecosystem completely."

"So that's why you want to negotiate," I said. "To stop it before it's too late."

"Yes," Tristan replied. "We talked about leaving, but our enchantment is connected to the island, and without it protecting us, there is nowhere in the sea we can go without being discovered. That's why we decided to try negotiations and sought out Sea Haven for support. I volunteered to organize a team to venture to Sea Haven, while Zale went undercover on the drillship to gather information. We did it in honor of our mother."

"Tristan, I'm so sorry," I whispered.

He cleared his throat. "You don't have to apologize. It's not your doing."

"But Ocean Rock isn't the only ones who have hurt your pod," I pointed out. "Sea Haven is responsible for the deaths of five mermen, and it's not right that even my people, who came from your pod, couldn't treat you with the dignity and respect you deserve."

Tristan reached out and took my hand. "I can't tell you how much I appreciate that you want to help. We're going to get through this and help save both our homes... together."

The way his eyes sparkled when he looked at me caused my heart to give a jolt in my chest. The connection we shared frightened me, and I yanked away. "We should probably be heading back."

Tristan furrowed his brow. "Did I say something wrong?"

"No, you said all the right things," I said flatly. "You always do."

"Then what is the matter?" he prodded, sounding so concerned for me when he did.

My mouth got me into a lot of trouble, but staying quiet wasn't working either. I tried to hold my words back, choking them down like Liana had insisted I do, but I couldn't stop the confession from tumbling out of me. "I don't know how to read you, Tristan. It feels like I found you on that beach for a reason, like your magic was calling out to me that night and hasn't stopped since. Maybe you're just being fun and welcoming, but to me I feel a connection, and I don't think this is appropriate given the circumstances."

"The circumstances?" he repeated.

Now I was just getting frustrated, because he couldn't possibly be this oblivious. "Tristan, I know you're engaged to Cordelia."

He reeled back, sinking several inches in the water. He wore a dumbfounded look, which irritated me. "Oh, I see. I, uh, should've mentioned that."

"Why didn't you?" I demanded. "I've been waiting for you to mention it, and you've never brought her up. It feels weird that I had to hear it from your fiancé when you and I have been spending so much time together."

"You're right," he said. "I should've mentioned it. It's my mistake."

"That's not an explanation, Tristan," I stated firmly. "You didn't tell me you were a prince. You didn't tell me you were betrothed. You don't owe me anything, but if we're going to work together I need to understand you."

"I apologize I wasn't forthcoming about this information, but it was never my intention to hide myself from you. In the Luna pod, these things are a given."

"So, it wasn't intentional, only a miscommunication?" I asked skeptically, though Tristan sounded genuine.

"We've brought a lot of things back from the surface, but the monarchy is one thing that hasn't changed," Tristan explained. "I told you how important the queen's role is. Therefore, historically Luna royals are betrothed from a young age and set to marry in their early twenties. I failed to recognize that you wouldn't understand our royal customs, and I shouldn't have made assumptions. For that, I am truly sorry."

Internally, I felt wholly conflicted because this didn't feel real... *he* didn't feel real. He was being too genuine, too kind, and while I wanted to trust him and believe such kindness existed in the world, I couldn't fathom how this could all go over his head. He was feeding me half-truths, and I struggled to comprehend why he couldn't just be upfront with me.

"So what is... *this*?" I asked sharply, gesturing between the two of us. "Another cultural difference I'm misinterpreting? Back home when you're constantly taking someone's hand and winking at them, and you *never* mention the person you're supposed to be marrying... it looks a whole lot like flirting."

I expected Tristan to push back, to deny it and tell me that's how friends acted in the Luna pod. Instead, he swayed his fins and backed away a few inches. "I'm here to be your mentor, and that's it. The rest of it never should've happened. I will keep my distance from now on, if that is what you wish."

"What I wish is that I didn't have to explain why this is a problem, because it isn't fair to me, and it certainly isn't fair to your fiancé. Maybe it *is* best if we keep our distance." I spun around and started out the way we came.

"Wait," Tristan called once we emerged from the shipwreck.

I whirled back around. "Wait for what, Tristan? For my siren song to echo to the trench and back? For my mermaid tail to manifest? Where is that getting us? I've been waiting around for someone to *do* something. Meanwhile, I don't know if my family's even still *alive* back in Sea Haven. I want to help the Luna pod, but I don't know how much longer I can wait at the expense of my own people. I'll find my mertail on my own, and you can go back to your perfect life in the palace."

Tristan scoffed, shaking his head. "Perfect? Did you not listen to everything I just told you? You're enchanted by shimmering scales and glowing caverns, but things in the Luna pod are far from perfect. You really want to see how perfect the Luna pod is? Follow me."

This time, Tristan didn't extend his hand. He spun around and flicked his fins to distance himself from me. I hesitated. I knew my accusation was out of line, and I already wished I could take it back.

Tristan paused to shoot a glance over his shoulder. "Well?" he pressed. "Do you want to see the truth for yourself or not?"

CHAPTER 14

My curiosity got the better of me, and I followed behind Tristan, keeping a fair amount of distance between us.

We swam for miles in silence. The ocean floor became bare of life, and the water was so murky I could hardly see Tristan ahead of me. The sea seemed thicker here, like swimming through soup, and even though I inhaled saltwater, it felt like I wasn't getting enough oxygen.

Finally, Tristan stopped and turned to me, his usual shiny scales barely discernible in the dim light. He spread his arms wide. "You see what they've done? You call this perfect?"

My guts twisted. "This is the mining site?"

"Yes, and it just keeps getting worse."

"I don't understand how they can get away with this. Someone ashore should be regulating what they're doing here."

"Who's going to know if they don't report their mistakes?" Tristan asked rhetorically. "They don't care what they destroy to get what they want."

I swallowed a lump rising in my throat, because these people were no different than the former Sea Haven council head Carson Ray. He was more than willing to take from innocent people to get the resources he wanted. It was so wrong.

Tristan gestured for me to follow. "Come see this."

I stayed close at his side so I wouldn't lose him. We swam until we came upon a large pipe secured to the ocean floor. I turned my gaze upward, following the pipe all the way to the surface. I could just barely make out the shadow of a large ship high above us.

"It's bigger than I thought it'd be," I remarked. "I've never seen anything like it."

"There's more," Tristan said.

He started swimming upward, and I kicked my feet to ascend behind him. The higher we went, the bigger the ship appeared, until I was reeling at its sheer size. It had to be nearly a thousand feet long. We were close enough now that I could see the propellers on the bottom of the ship that kept the massive structure in place.

Our heads broke the surface of the water. I craned my

neck to take in the height of the ship. The drillship was red, with a black half-circle logo and the words *Ocean Rock* beneath it. I was unfamiliar with the logo, but already it left a bad taste in my mouth.

Tristan tapped my shoulder. When I turned, my stomach lurched. The drillship wasn't the only piece of equipment on the water. There was also a large platform that looked to be constructed entirely of metal, equipped with cranes that reached high into the air. We could hear the voices of the men on deck shouting instructions at each other as they worked to assemble the platform into place.

"That must be the permanent structure you mentioned," I noted. It was hard to comprehend the sheer amount of planning and money that went into something like that.

"Can you imagine what would happen if their equipment fails?" Tristan asked.

"It'd be... catastrophic," I said hollowly, before dropping my head. "I never should've said your life was perfect. I know you've lost a lot and came to Sea Haven for a reason. You never would've done that unless you were desperate to help your people. I can tell you really care about them, and being a prince must be a huge responsibility. You seem to handle it really well, but just because you make it look easy doesn't mean it isn't difficult. That kind of position should come with respect, not accusations. I'm sorry."

"I too am sorry," he replied kindly. "I should never assume you and I are working with the same information.

It's difficult to see the impact Ocean Rock has made on our city when you have nothing to compare it to."

"To think that Luna City was even more beautiful than it is now is hard to comprehend, because it already seems like a dream. I can't imagine it being destroyed. But Tristan, I'm terrified for your people. These rigs are huge investments, costing multiple millions of dollars. Humans can be extremely cruel and selfish when it comes to money, and they aren't going to give up that kind of investment easily. They don't even care that they're hurting the ocean life. I know you think you can reason with them, but they won't negotiate and abandon this platform. They'll squeeze every last bit of life from this place, like Carson did with our magic back in Sea Haven."

"We have to at least try..." Tristan insisted, but he trailed off as the sound of helicopter blades stole our attention from overhead.

I looked upward, and what I saw made my heart drop all the way to the ocean floor. On the side of the helicopter was a blue logo hooked on the end like an ocean wave. The helicopter began to descend toward a landing platform on the drillship. I grabbed Tristan and yanked him under the water, kicking my scuba fins to get far away from the surface as quickly as possible.

"What is it?" Tristan demanded.

"We have to go," I panicked. "I've seen that logo before. That's the Blue Wave Energy logo."

Tristan paused, and his features paled as recognition

set in. "The company your council runs that's stealing your people's magic?"

He already knew the answer, but like me, he was trying to wrap his head around the fact that they were *here*.

My stomach knotted as I turned to face him. "Yes, but I don't understand. I thought Blue Wave Energy and Ocean Rock were two different companies. Something's very wrong here."

Tristan ran his fingers through his beard. "I agree. We need to—"

He was cut off as a shadow descended upon him, enveloping him from every angle before either of us knew what was happening. Tristan thrashed, and I cried out and lunged forward to find my fingers tangled in a fishing net. The horrible realization that he was being captured—and what those aboard the drillship would do to him—sent my heart pummeling against my rib cage.

"Tristan!" I screamed, yanking as hard as I could on the net to try to break him free, but the rope only cut my fingers. I ignored the pain and pulled harder, until blood began swirling out of my fingers and into the water.

Tristan pulled on the net, trying to find an opening, but the more we wrenched on the ropes, the more tangled he became. The net began to ascend toward the drillship, and my stomach lurched.

"No!" I cried.

Tristan reached his fingers through the net to touch mine. "I'll find a way to escape. I'll use my siren call to compel them, and they'll forget they ever saw me."

"Not if Blue Wave brought a piece of their sea stone!" I insisted.

Rage filled me from head to toe, and it seemed to take no effort to connect with the sea and *beg* her not to let any harm come to one of her own. An immense desire to protect that which I cared about caused storm clouds to brew overhead, leaving us in near darkness within moments. I recalled everything I learned that day near the cove, summoning every ounce of power within me to command the sea's raging waves.

Currents came rushing in from all directions as I commanded the water to attack the net, hoping enough pressure would snap the rope. But the water merely filtered through the net, doing no damage at all.

"It's no use," Tristan insisted.

"I won't let them hurt you again," I demanded. "I'm getting you out of here."

I had to think *fast*. I had no weapons, and the little magic I had access to was no help here. I kicked my feet, using everything within me to force a strong current at my back that thrust me toward the ocean floor. The water was immensely deep here, and every second I took diving downward took me farther away from Tristan.

My hands met the ocean floor, digging into the sand until my fingers clamped around a sharp rock that fit in my palm. I had no time to question if it would get the job done; I just had to make it work.

I planted my heels into the sand, then kicked off the bottom of the ocean and shot toward the surface. I could see Tristan's shadow tangled in the net, rising higher and higher. He was nearly to the surface when I reached him. I grabbed tight to the net, then sliced the rock as hard as I could against the ropes. A hole tore through the net.

Tristan shoved his hands through the tear, pulling it wider while I cut more ropes with the rock. The top of the net rose above the surface of the water. We were so close that I could hear voices from above us.

"I think we got a big one!" someone shouted.

Heart hammering, I feared we wouldn't make it before they dragged him aboard. Then, to my immense relief, we gained enough leverage to tear the hole wide enough for Tristan to slip through.

Tristan grabbed my hand. "Go!"

I kicked my flippers, and a massive current spun through the water at my command to carry us far from the surface and away from the drillship. Tristan flicked his fins so hard that we moved through the water faster than I'd ever swam before, until we were far outside the range of the ship and couldn't see it anymore.

Tristan and I collapsed beside each other on the ocean floor, both panting and out of breath. Without giving it a second thought, I threw my arms over his chest, burying my face in his shoulder.

"I thought they were going to take you again!" I cried.

Tristan placed a gentle hand on my back, relaxing into the sand. "Never."

My head snapped upward. "Your brother's on that boat! Whoever was on that helicopter has to be from the

Sea Haven Council. If they find out that Zale's from the Luna pod, he could be in danger."

Tristan sprang upright, facing back toward the drillship. "We must warn him."

I grabbed Tristan's shoulder to stop him. "We don't stand a chance without help. We have to go alert your father."

Tristan hesitated, then nodded. "All right, but let's move quickly."

We raced back to Luna City, and the guards at the palace let us straight through. We found King Aalto in the throne room, surrounded by his council members. I didn't catch what they were discussing before we barged in.

"There's a situation at the drillship," I blurted.

King Aalto's features paled when he noticed the cuts on my fingers, and he sprang up out of his throne. "Are we under attack?"

"Not yet," Tristan said. "But you're going to want to see this."

King Aalto followed, along with his council members and guards. We explained on the way about the helicopter we'd seen, as well as how Tristan had been caught in the net.

"If these two companies are associated, this can't mean anything but bad news," King Aalto worried.

We reached the outskirts of the mining area and swam to the surface. This far out on the open water, no one would be able to see us from the ship. But we could see them—their ship, their platform...

And their empty helipad.

I glanced toward the skies, which were now clear of the storm I'd conjured. We could see all the way to the horizon, but there was no sign of the helicopter we'd seen.

I furrowed my brow. "I don't understand. We weren't gone that long. I don't know why they'd come here just to leave immediately."

"You're *sure* it was your council?" King Aalto questioned.

I hesitated. "We didn't see who was aboard, but I know that logo. Tristan saw it, too."

"It did look similar to the symbols I saw when I was in Sea Haven," he agreed.

A distant voice carried through the water.

King Aalto turned toward the sound. "Is that Zale?"

"He must've realized the same thing we did and fled," I said.

We ducked back underwater and could hear Zale's voice coming closer. "Who's out here?"

"It's us," Tristan called. "We're over here."

Zale swam closer, his red scales shimmering off the light near the surface. He looked surprised to see his father and his guards. "What's going on?"

"You don't know?" Tristan asked.

Zale shook his head. "A few guys were fishing off the rig and their net broke. They said a fish must've chewed through it, but I knew when I saw those cuts that they weren't marks from any fish. I knew it was a merfolk, but I couldn't figure out what anyone would be doing this close to the rig. I came to check they were all right."

"It was me," Tristan said. "I brought Bree to show her what we were up against. She deserved to know. Thankfully, we got away, but not before we saw the helicopter."

Zale's eyebrows pinched together. "The supply copter? What does that have to do with anything?"

"It wasn't just any supply drop," I insisted. "That helicopter came from Sea Haven. Have you ever seen that particular helicopter here before—the one with the blue logo?"

"Blue logo?" Zale asked. "No, it was a red helicopter doing a routine supply drop, like normal."

King Aalto swam between us. "What exactly is going on here? Is the Sea Haven Council here or not?"

"Yes," I said, the same time Zale answered, "No."

Zale turned to his father. "I'm doing everything I can on that boat to gather information and ensure we're all safe. I think I would've noticed if other merfolk showed up."

"Or the truth is being hidden from you," I argued.

Zale sighed. "If that's the case, then it's my job to uncover the truth, so I need to get back there and make sure there are no other merfolk aboard that ship. And if there are... well, maybe it's time to move ashore anyway."

Zale's shoulders fell, like he was beginning to lose hope that the Luna pod would ever defeat Ocean Rock and remove them from their waters.

"We won't so much as entertain that notion," King

Aalto bellowed. "I fear you've been spending too much time on the surface. If this has become too much for you, I'll send someone else to do your job."

"No, I want to do this," Zale said. "I can help the Luna pod, and it was hard enough to get me aboard and build trust with the crew in the first place."

"Zale, you could be in danger," I told him.

"You're all in danger the longer you stay here, but not from the Sea Haven Council that's hundreds of miles away on the mainland," Zale insisted. "You have Ocean Rock to worry about, and if you're not careful, they could spot you and we'll all be exposed to this crew."

"My son is right," King Aalto agreed. "Their equipment could spot us, and the longer Zale's off that ship, the more suspicious it looks. Sitting around speculating without definitive proof is a waste of our time."

"I'm on the clock right now, and my absence will be noticed if I'm gone too long," Zale said. "I'll keep an eye out for any mention of visitors from Sea Haven, but I'm afraid this may be a misunderstanding."

"What if I'm correct, and the Sea Haven Council is here? What do we do when they discover you?" I demanded.

"Then we retaliate," King Aalto said. "But not before we can confirm what you claim you saw. Zale will return to the ship and alert us immediately if he hears anything about Sea Haven or Blue Wave Energy. In the meantime..." He turned to us. "You two put yourselves and the entire Luna Pod at risk by coming here."

"But Father—" Tristan started to explain.

King Aalto raised a hand to stop him. "I don't want to hear it, Tristan. You came out here without considering how this could affect the pod. You claim to be ready to take over as king, but you have yet to show me that you have what it takes. You will return to Luna City with me, and you won't come back here again unless under my explicit orders."

Tristan nodded. "Yes, Father."

I couldn't believe King Aalto was brushing this off so easily. A hundred insults sat on my tongue, but King Aalto turned before I could respond. He swam away in such a commanding manner, his shoulders back, that all the guards followed immediately.

I gritted my teeth as Tristan and I trailed behind them. "Your father's wrong to brush this off."

Tristan lowered his voice, so only I could hear. "You think Zale's lying?"

"I think he's mistaken, and he doesn't have access to as much information on that ship as he believes."

Tristan shot a glance ahead toward the king, but kept his voice quiet. "My father has become a cautious man after what happened to my mother. He is not willing to put his people at risk without having all the information laid out for him."

"He's not being cautious enough by sending Zale back there," I insisted. "The fact is, I don't think your father believes me. But you saw that Blue Wave Energy logo."

Tristan nodded. "I did, but... we only caught a glimpse. Are we *certain* of what we saw?"

I frowned. "That logo sits outside City Hall. I always thought it was our city's logo, until we broke in and discovered what they're doing behind the scenes. Believe me, Tristan. I've seen that logo a million times. Ocean Rock may not have known about the merfolk's existence before, but we can't assume to know what information they're operating with anymore. The Sea Haven Council is up to something. I just don't know what they're planning, or how long they've been planning it. But I know one thing for sure. No matter how pretty it looks on the outside, Sea Haven wasn't safe for my people, and Luna City is no longer safe for yours."

Problem was, if I couldn't get the king to listen to me, how could I expect to keep anyone else safe?

CHAPTER 15

The fall equinox had arrived, when the day and night were equal lengths, and it was a big deal in the Luna pod. In the days when seafolk were still navigating the seas, the seasonal shift marked a key reference point for mapping the stars. The Luna pod still celebrated the changing seasons and the transition to autumn constellations. It was also the annual tradition of reinforcing the protection enchantment on the island, which everyone in the pod participated in.

The festivities began at sundown, when thousands of merfolk gathered at the surface to celebrate beneath the stars. Liana and I surfaced near Crystal Cove, where Tristan had taken me my first day of training.

The cove, the nearby beach, and the open waters beyond felt like a completely different place than it had that day I summoned a storm. When Tristan first brought me here, the cove was quiet and secluded. Now it was filled with lively chatter and groups of merfolk splashing around.

Zale had managed to slip away from his duties aboard the drillship for the occasion, and Liana quickly found him through the crowd.

"Zale!" she called, waving at him as she bobbed up and down on the surface.

The prince wore a bright smile and made his way over to us. "I was hoping I'd find you here."

"Where else would we be?" Liana teased. "I'm so glad you were able to get off that ship for the night."

Zale draped an arm around her shoulder, and Liana clung to him. "I wouldn't miss it," he said smoothly, his eyes sparkling down at her.

The two of them hadn't been able to stop staring at each other since we arrived in Luna City. I was certain Liana had already fallen madly in love with him.

"Any updates for us?" I asked Zale.

He shook his head regrettably. "I'm afraid I don't have any news about what you saw. I haven't seen any strangers aboard the drillship, and there are no whispers of Blue Wave Energy or Sea Haven among the crew."

I was starting to wonder if Zale had been right and I'd

merely witnessed a routine supply drop. It was starting to look more plausible that I'd only imagined that logo on the side of the helicopter.

"Let's not concern ourselves with such problems tonight," Zale suggested. "The equinox is a time of celebration! Come, and let us release our worries of seasons past."

Zale led us out of the open ocean and into Crystal Cove, where merfolk perched upon the rocks circling the perimeter, their fins resting in the water. We found an empty spot to sit, and Liana unfurled her golden fins over the rocks while I climbed higher to peer into the waters below. I maneuvered carefully so I wouldn't trip on my scuba fins, then draped my skirt over my legs when I sat. When Tristan and I first visited this place, the waters were calm and crystal clear, but on the night of the autumn equinox, the cove had been transformed into a swirling whirlpool.

Sanvi, the spiritual leader of the pod, sat near the waterfall singing an ancient song. With her arms in the air and chin lifted toward the stars, she commanded the water to spiral downward like a draining sink. Merfolk whispered prayers, then tossed offerings into a spinning vortex, where they circled the cove a few times before being sucked into the waters below.

"What's the significance of the whirlpool?" Liana asked Zale.

"It's an ancient seafolk tradition," the prince explained. "The autumn equinox is a time for releasing the things that are no longer serving you, expressing gratitude, and honoring our ancestors. The Luna pod combines traditions from around the world to welcome in a time of reflection as we enter the darker months."

"That's so beautiful," Liana raved, though she wasn't looking at the vortex anymore. Instead, she was batting her eyelashes at Zale.

The prince reached out to brush her wet hair out of her eyes. "It's a time to release stuck energy, to be present in nature, and to honor the balance between the light and the dark, so that we can move forward into the darker months."

Liana sighed blissfully and leaned into Zale's arms. "So poetic."

I didn't know if Zale was blowing smoke out his ass, but it sounded like he was putting on a show for her. Liana seemed wholly entranced by it.

"Where do the offerings go?" I asked.

Zale turned toward me. "There's an underwater tunnel that connects the cove to another part of the city. Sanvi uses her powers to create a channel that sends all the offerings through the tunnel and into the Ancestral Trench."

Maybe Zale wasn't completely full of it. Tristan had explained the significance of the trench to me before, and how the Kraken consumed the pod's memories. It made sense the creature would accept their equinox offerings as well.

"What kind of offerings should we make?" Liana asked.

Zale shrugged. "Anything you'd like that represents something you're letting go of. You can use rocks, shells, leaves, feathers—even a scale off your own fins. Once your offering is complete, we'll head to the beach where we will moonbathe."

"Ooh, what's that?" Liana practically sang.

"It's a cleansing ritual, using the light of the moon to clear old energy from our bodies and realign ourselves," Zale explained.

"Is there a special way to perform these rituals?" Liana wondered.

"It's quite simple—just choose an object to represent your desires, state your intentions, and release it. Allow me to demonstrate." Zale withdrew a tiny shimmering gem that had been tucked beneath one of his scales. "This gem represents my childhood. I grew up thinking I was just one thing—a prince of the merfolk. But like this gem, we are all multi-faceted, and while I will always be a prince, I wish to become far more. And so, I am releasing the belief that I have to be just one thing, and welcoming everything I can become—both as part of that identity, and outside of it. I am not only a prince, but an explorer, a visionary, and even a lover. I am ready to become the *man* I'm meant to be."

Liana never took her eyes off him, clinging to his every word. I felt like I shouldn't be watching, because clearly his speech was meant entirely for her.

Zale tossed his gem into the water, and it shimmered in the moonlight for a moment before being swept up in the current and swirling downward into Sanvi's vortex.

Then he leaned back, putting one arm around Liana. "What will you release, my dear?"

Liana giggled at the pet name, batting her eyelashes at him once again. Thank god I was sitting behind them, because it took me a few moments to notice my distaste was written all over my face. Could they at least save their ridiculous flirting for later?

I caught myself and quickly righted my features.

Liana leaned over and plucked one of her shimmering golden scales from her tail, wincing as it broke free. She curled the scale tightly in her hand. "This scale is a symbol of the new me, the mermaid who gets to explore a whole new world and become everything she desires. I'm not letting go of her, but releasing everything I used to be so that I can *become* her."

Liana tossed the scale into the water, and it floated on the surface before being swept away by the current. A pang of melancholy struck me in the chest as I watched it go. It felt sad to witness her release even *one* single scale, as if each one wasn't as precious as the last. If it were me, no one would be able to pry a scale from my fins that easily, not even a handsome royal prince.

"Your turn, Bree," Liana said cheerfully.

She gazed up at me expectantly, but I hadn't decided yet what I was going to release. "You guys go on ahead of me," I suggested. "I'll probably be a while."

"Are you sure?" Liana asked, sounding concerned.

"Yeah, I need to meditate on it for a bit." I waved toward the beach. "Enjoy your moonbathing."

"All right, we'll see you later." Liana waved goodbye, then jumped into the water with Zale and swam off toward the beach, splashing each other playfully as they went.

In their absence, I climbed down the rocks closer to the water, sticking my legs in. All around me, merfolk whispered prayers and tossed their equinox offerings into the cove, but I merely sat still. I knew there were things I had to let go of, but articulating exactly what those things were didn't come easily. I often acted upon impulse and wasn't the kind of girl to sit there contemplating in silence. The longer I thought about it, the heavier my shoulders felt, as if there was a weight bearing down on me.

Well, that was *one* thing I could certainly let go of.

If all the other merfolk could do this ceremony, then I wanted to try it. I reached for a small rock nearby, curling it in my hands as I placed them over my heart. I inhaled a deep breath of salty air while I listened to Sanvi's melody and focused on the cool breeze passing through my hair.

"This rock represents the weight of all that's holding me back," I whispered to myself. "I release this weight on my shoulders, so I may enter the new season light and free to explore the pieces of myself I'm still missing."

I tossed the rock into the cove, but instead of joining with the other offerings in the vortex, I watched the rock sink to the bottom. I sighed at the irony.

"Is this seat taken?" a voice asked from my right.

I jumped a little as Tristan pulled himself out of the water and onto the rock beside me. His long green fins spread across the rocks. I nudged him with my shoulder. "Don't sneak up on me like that. You scared me!"

"Scaring you is the last thing I wish to do. It's supposed to be a night of peace."

I pulled my feet from the water, curling my knees closer to my chest. "I'd hoped to find some peace, but my offering sank to the bottom."

Tristan frowned. "Something on your mind?"

"I'm trying to do that whole letting-go thing, but I can't quite figure out what's bothering me," I admitted. I was conflicted about opening up to him completely, but the words seemed to tumble out of me. It was clear I was more comfortable around Tristan than I cared to admit, but I didn't think he noticed.

"It's okay if it takes you some time," he encouraged. "The autumn equinox is a time to pause and remember that as one thing ends, another begins. We are here to release the old and ground ourselves for the coming months of darkness, so that we can spend that time self-reflecting. There is wisdom in letting go, in order to welcome renewal, but it is not a process one can rush."

That weight on my shoulder seemed to respond to Tristan's words, nudging it ever so slightly away. Zale had seemed full of it when he was describing the ritual significance to Liana, but Tristan made it all sound important and powerful.

"I guess Zale and Liana made it look easy, like you should just intuitively *know* what you want and where to go next," I remarked.

Tristan eyed me curiously. "Does it bother you seeing my brother and your best friend together?"

I wanted to say no, because I'd never seen Liana so happy and I wanted the best for her, but the word caught on my tongue. A bitter taste filled my mouth, and I realized why their obnoxious flirting had been bothering me.

"Oh, my god," I breathed. "It's like you can read my mind. I'm jealous, aren't I?"

Tristan tilted his head. "You tell me."

"I must be," I mused. "Liana offered one of her scales in the ritual, and when she did that, I felt my heart drop. As happy as I am for her, it feels like I'm watching her get everything I don't get to have. I had my core taken from me, and without my siren call or mertail, I can't seem to forget what that felt like, when it seems so easy for her. It's not fair of me to feel this way, because Liana's magic has been suppressed her whole life, too. Plus, I'm the one who dragged her into all of this, and she's been forced from her home as well."

"You just want what she has, which is valid," Tristan said.

"I guess so, but I don't want to be jealous of it. That feels so... icky. I'm really happy that she's able to summon her tail, and she's found someone that lights her up, so whatever this is, I need to get over it."

"Are you worried you can't have what she has?" Tristan wondered.

I stared into the whirlpool, thinking hard. "I don't know. I think I'm more worried about what it will take for me to get there."

"It's important to remember that we're all riding our

own current through life," Tristan said. "What Liana's accomplished by summoning her tail stands a symbol of what's possible for you, too."

"You're right," I agreed. "Which is why I'm going to release this jealousy, because that's the absolute *last* thing that's going to help me. I can't expect to walk other people's path and think it's going to lead me to where I need to go. I've got to figure out where my path leads. Maybe I don't know what the path ahead looks like, but perhaps if I just put one foot in front of the other, I'll get where I need to go."

I picked up another rock, then threw it as far as I could toward the vortex. The spiraling water caught it, and it went spinning downward with the other offerings. The air in my chest certainly felt lighter once it was gone.

I turned to Tristan. "Thanks. Your insight is always super helpful."

He smiled. "That's what mentors are for."

Right. He was my *mentor* and nothing more.

I gestured to his closed fist. "What's your offering?"

Tristan unfurled his fingers to reveal a smooth, shimmering white pearl.

I gasped at its unmatched beauty. "Tristan, it's perfect."

"That's the idea. This equinox, I wish to let go of the need to be perfect in every way. I'm a prince, and that can come with the pressure to be perfect in every moment, to always say the right thing and present myself in just the right manner to earn the people's respect. But I want to be the kind of prince who's allowed to make mistakes, and still be seen for the good in me. So... here's to making all kinds of silly mistakes."

Tristan drew his arm back, but instead of tossing the pearl into the water, it slipped out of his fingers and bounced on the rocks.

I laughed. "It looks like the mistakes have already begun."

Tristan smiled as he caught the pearl before it bounced into the water. "The first mistake of many, which makes it almost too *perfect*... Isn't that exactly what I was trying to avoid?"

I smirked. "I guess you're just going to have to practice not being so dang perfect."

I couldn't help the jibe from slipping out of me. It was certainly not something you should say to your mentor, but maybe I could settle with teasing a *friend*.

Tristan grinned as he tossed his hair over his shoulder, playing along. "But it's hard when it's so *natural*."

I playfully shoved him, and he lost his balance on the rocks and slid into the water.

"Hey!" Tristan quickly resurfaced and tossed his hair out of his eyes. "*I'm* the one who's supposed to be making the mistakes here."

I flicked a few droplets of water into his face. "So what are you waiting for then, fish boy?"

"Absolutely nothing." Tristan grabbed my ankle before he finished speaking, then yanked me into the water. My laughter turned into bubbles as my head dipped below the surface.

The sound of a blaring conch shell cut me off, and we both turned in the direction of the sound. All around us, merfolk jumped off the rocks and into the water and began swimming out of the cove.

"What's that?" I asked.

Tristan wore a bright smile, his eyes twinkling in the moonlight. "It's the best part of the night. Come on."

CHAPTER 16

I followed alongside Tristan as he started behind the others and out of the cove.

"It's time to sing Melodia, our enchanting song," Tristan explained. "The pod will gather on the beach now, and the monarchy will lead the call to reinforce our enchantment on the island."

"How does enchanting work?"

"It's a form of siren compulsion that's achieved when a large group of merfolk come together. When the song is led by a trusted leader, and all the pod joins their voices together, it creates a potent vibration that can be infused into sentimental objects—or in our case this landmark.

Usually, the enchantment is led by the queen, but this year my father will be leading us for the first time."

"So enchanting can only be done in large groups?" I asked.

"There are different forms of siren enchantment," Tristan said. "In ancient times, merfolk used to enchant bottles to be carried across the ocean current to get messages from one pod to another. A simple enchantment like that could be done by an individual. This type of protection enchantment, however, is more powerful and long-lasting, so it requires a group effort. Each time we add our voices to the ancient song of our ancestors, our protection spell grows stronger. You'll see. There's nothing quite like it."

We reached the beach, where Tristan left my side to go gather with the monarchs, while I went to join the rest of the pod. Colorful fins unfurled over the sand everywhere I looked. I glanced around for Liana and Zale, but the beach was so crowded that I didn't see them. Instead, I took a seat in the sand by myself, facing the water like the others were doing.

Once the pod had congregated on the beach, a cyclone spiraled out of the sea and carried King Aalto upward so we could all see him. He held a trident glowing with bioluminescent algae, which illuminated his features in the darkness of night. His sonic scream projected his voice over the crowd.

"Welcome all to the autumn equinox ceremony!" he called. "As is our annual tradition, we will now sing the enchanting song of our ancestors, to infuse our island with our protection magic, so that no man nor ship may enter our waters, and that Luna City may continue to thrive in peace."

I could tell the king didn't fully believe his own words, but he didn't mention the drillship that was still stationed not far offshore. The last thing the king needed was to plant a seed of doubt in these people's minds and affect the spell they'd spent centuries upholding.

"We will begin with a moment of silence to honor Queen Lorelei, who has led us in singing Melodia for decades..." King Aalto trailed off.

While the other seafolk bowed their heads, I kept my eyes on the king. His mouth remained open, but nothing came out. It reminded me of the day at the memorial with Ronan's mother, how her grief had silenced her.

The moment of silence stretched on, and then a second column of water rose over the people. It carried Tristan upward, until he was at his father's side. Tristan looked different than he had minutes ago. He wore a golden crown embedded with gems that sparkled from afar, and he clutched a shiny gold trident in one hand. Tristan normally had this soft look about him, but in his prince attire, he looked positively fierce in a respectable way. Even his expression has changed. His usual delicate features appeared harder, as if his face had been carved from marble.

I admired him for how effortlessly he seemed to move

into his leadership role. The prince was absolutely breathtaking.

But different, too... prim, proper, nearly stiff. I didn't think anyone else noticed.

Tristan placed a gentle hand on his father's shoulder, then projected his voice over the beach. "My dearest Luna pod. Tonight is not only a night of celebration, but a time to give thanks to our ancestors, express gratitude, and let go of our worries of yesteryear. Together, we are united and strong. As we come together in song, let us remind ourselves that our voices are one with our ancestors who came before us, and will remain here with our descendants for years to come, for our impact, courage, and heart will always live on in the people we love."

It was the kind of speech Tristan would give to me in a quiet moment when we were alone. I'd never witnessed a display of his wisdom and caring heart in front of all his people. It was clear they had deep respect for him, and that he wanted nothing more than to keep his people safe and protected. His words were true, and I could feel them deep down into my core.

King Aalto clutched Tristan's shoulder tightly and cleared his throat. "Tonight, my eldest son, His Royal Highness Prince Tristan Adamaris, will lead the Luna pod in song."

Their exchange had been so quick and subtle that it appeared they'd been planning this all along. The rest of the pod didn't notice, but I recognized what Tristan had done. He'd stepped in to lead the pod when his father couldn't, and it took someone with a genuinely kind heart to do that.

Tristan opened his mouth, and by the Kraken himself, I'd never heard anything more beautiful. A low note emitted from his throat, echoing with a magical vibrato that sent tingles up and down my spine. My very bones seemed to resonate with his song.

Ancestral voices overlaying one another resounded from somewhere within the island, growing louder as the song of old harmonized with the beautiful notes Tristan sang. His voice rose and fell with the melody like calm ocean waves.

Tristan raised his trident, and the pod began to sing along. Thousands of voices joined in, and I expected it to be overpowering, but instead it was the calmest, most peaceful sound I'd heard in all my life. I wanted nothing more than to be a part of it.

I sat with my arms curled around my knees, eyes closed and just *listening* to the melody, to learn it before I joined in. Before I could begin singing, a bright light appeared, and I opened my eyes to see that a gentle aquamarine luminescence was building from beneath each merfolk's fins on the beach. The island was lighting up to the sound of their song, soaking in each note and filling with their compulsion and protection magic. Tristan hadn't been wrong when he said there was nothing quite like it.

The sand glowed everywhere I looked...

Everywhere but below me.

I glanced around frantically for answers, but the other

merfolk all had their eyes closed and were locked in embraces with their families, swaying back and forth and oblivious to the lone girl with her feet in the sand.

I glanced over the ocean toward Tristan, but my heart sank at what I saw. The cyclone that had lifted Tristan into the air was gone, and he'd returned to the water, where Cordelia was waiting at his side. She had one hand on the side of his face, staring deep into his eyes while she sang, as if she was singing just for him.

Then Tristan leaned in, and the couple connected in a long, passionate kiss.

The rock I'd thrown into the whirlpool might as well have come spinning right back out of the sea and down my throat, because I immediately choked on the note I was attempting to sing. Tristan had helped me release some of my fears in the cove, but now they came rushing back like a tidal wave. I shouldn't feel this way—I didn't *want* to feel this way. Like Tristan said, we all had our own path to follow, and clearly he wasn't mine. The pale patch of sand beneath me made me wonder if the Luna pod was a part of my path at all.

Another pair of feet appeared before me, and it took me a second to realize that they shouldn't be there. We were on land, but I hadn't seen one single person shift out of their fins.

I lifted my gaze to see Noah peering down at me with a bright smile. "Need some company?"

Despite the glowing sand around me, Noah was like a beacon glowing brighter than all the rest of the island, drawing me in. Suddenly, I didn't feel so alone anymore, and the initial panic that had set in washed away.

I nodded. "Yes, please."

Noah sat beside me in the sand, then offered his hand to me. "Sing with me?"

"I want to," I told him. "But I'm... scared."

"Of what?" he asked curiously.

I hesitated, until I noticed the sand beneath me began glowing in his presence. I didn't know what it meant, but I knew it had to be significant.

"I don't know," I admitted. "That I'll get the song wrong."

"Then follow me," he offered. "I'd never lead you astray."

"Okay." I entwined my fingers with his, and Noah's beautiful siren voice began to swell over me like a warm embrace.

I began to sing. Though my notes didn't match perfectly with the song, I kept up as best I could, and the weight I'd been holding on to all night seemed to lift. I leaned my head against Noah's shoulder, and he began to rock us back and forth.

Being this close to Noah felt intimate and welcoming. I thought of the conversation Tristan and I had in the cove, and how my path would unfold before me. I wanted to be a part of all of this, but regardless of where the journey took me, I'd always intended for it to lead me back home.

Perhaps the best thing I could do was stop fighting the current, and let it take me where I was meant to go.

CHAPTER 17

As the song faded and the ceremony came to an end, I found myself curling closer to Noah, burying my head in his shoulder. I didn't want to leave his side just yet. The equinox gave me far more to think about than when the night began, and I needed more time to sort it all out.

"I'm ready to go," I told Noah. "Do you want to come with me?"

"Yeah, let's go," he said, though I knew I didn't even have to ask.

Noah accompanied me back to the lagoon, as he did every night since we'd been here. It'd become our routine, and something I looked forward to daily. The lagoon was far on the other side of the island from the festivities, tucked away in a private, secluded area that felt like ours alone. When I was here with Noah, I didn't have to worry about the conflicts that existed in the waters beyond. I could just *be* with my friend, with no expectations or pressure.

Noah and I climbed onto the deck of our boat, where he used his powers to command the water from our clothes, though I still shivered in the cool night air.

"Are you doing all right?" he asked.

I crossed my arms to ward off the chill. "Just cold."

"I know what will help—a warm shower and a hot meal. I'll get started on the food while you clean up," he offered. Noah was already moving toward the kitchenette before I could respond.

I ran my fingers through my hair and could feel the salt build-up. Thankfully, the small bathroom in the cabin had a shower, so I gathered my things and washed up. When I finished showering, I changed into dry sweatpants and an oversized tee and left my skirt to hang dry. It was only when I was with Noah that I felt like I could take that skirt off and be myself.

I emerged from the cabin and onto the deck to find Noah gone. I glanced over the water and noticed an orange glow from ashore. In the light of dancing flames, I could see Noah collecting sticks from the tree line. He'd started a fire on the beach, which looked warm and cozy.

In our time in Luna City, my connection to the ocean

had grown so strong that I could control the water with greater precision and ease. I commanded the sea to rise before me, and I stepped into the water, getting only my feet wet as water rushed upward to balance me. It was like walking on the surface as the ocean carried me to shore. I commanded the sea to set me gently in the sand and ordered the last of the water droplets to fall away, leaving me completely dry.

Noah knelt beside the coals, propping up sticks that had been skewered through fish he'd caught. He must've found seasonings on the boat, because the fish were already prepared with spices, which smelled rich and savory as they cooked.

He glanced over his shoulder when he heard me approaching. A wide smile spread across his face. "How do you like roasted fish?"

"It sounds delicious." I inhaled deeply. The pleasant scent brought back memories of home, which made the weight of the autumn equinox ceremony seem distant. I could easily imagine I was on Sea Haven Beach, the delicious smells from Sal's Sea Shack wafting down the beach. "And *smells* amazing."

A blanket lay in the sand, and I sat upon it, rubbing my palms together to warm them against the fire.

Noah dusted off his hands, then came to sit beside me. "It's not Sal's surf and turf, but it's the best I can do."

"Sal's surf and turf is the best!" I raved. "The restaurant's only a block from our house, so my parents and I used to go all the time. It's a Sea Haven classic."

"Absolutely," Noah agreed. "We used to order whole lobsters on special occasions. I loved that place so much that I got a job in the kitchen the summer before my senior year. Sal taught me all his secret recipes."

"Is this one of them?" I asked, gesturing to the fish cooking over the fire.

"It's as close as I can get." Noah lifted one of the sticks and twisted it around to check the fish from every angle. It looked roasted to perfection. "Here, you get the first bite. Let me know if I need to change anything."

Noah placed the fish on a plate, then removed the roasting stick. He handed me the plate and a fork, and I worked to peel the skin back and find a fleshy piece that flaked away from the bone.

I popped the meat into my mouth, and my eyes rolled back as savory flavors burst over my tongue. I couldn't cook to save my life, so Noah's skills impressed me. "Oh, my god. This might be *better* than Sal's."

Noah cocked an eyebrow. "No one's fish is better than Sal's."

I swallowed another delicious bite. "Well, you could give him a run for his money. If you develop your own recipes, you might put Sal out of business."

Noah laughed as he plated his own fish. "Sal's been talking about retirement for years. Maybe once all this is over, I could buy the place from him."

"Is that what you want?" I asked. "To own a restaurant?"

Noah laid on the blanket, propping himself up on one

elbow as he picked at his fish. "I used to think about it, before I left Sea Haven. There's nothing that brings people together quite like food. I learned that from my dad. Before I could even walk, he'd strap me to his chest and take me fishing. It was always a good day when we caught enough fish to filet and bring home to Mom, who was always ready with a new recipe. That was our thing, having a good time on the water, then singing and dancing around the kitchen."

Noah took a bite, then continued. "When I lost my parents, those were the memories I held on to the most, so sharing that joy with other people naturally seems like the best way to give back. I just never believed I could really make it happen, you know? You need money to buy a restaurant, and who's going to give a business loan to me?"

I shrugged. "They give out student loans to people our age all the time."

Noah chuckled as he swallowed another bite of fish. "Fair, but business loans are different. I need a whole business plan, and I don't know if I'm a business kind of guy."

I cocked an eyebrow. "And you think Sal is?"

Sal was an older guy who didn't know how to run the cash register at his own restaurant, but the man sure knew how to prepare seafood. That, along with his cheerful laugh that made his whole belly shake when he came out of the kitchen to greet regulars, is what kept people coming back.

Noah nodded. "Good point. Sal wouldn't be able to run that place without his partner Benham. Have you ever seen that man's office? He's got receipts stacked up taller than I am, but he can pull out a specific file at a moment's notice. He's got a system he knows like the back of his hand. I guess if Sal and Benham can run a restaurant, I can learn how to do it."

"I think you can do anything you put your mind to," I said. "If you want to open a restaurant, you should do it."

Noah lifted his gaze, staring up at me past long lashes. My heart gave a stutter, but I shoved that feeling down with a final bite of fish. I quickly cleared my throat and set my plate aside.

Noah glanced at the scraps of our dinner with a contemplative look. "Do you ever feel bad about eating fish?"

I shook my head. "I've thought about it before, because we're so close to sea life, but then I think about how fish eat other fish, and I figure it's the natural cycle of things. We just have to honor other ocean life, not be wasteful of it, and give back as much as we take."

"I couldn't agree more." A smile touched Noah's lips as he sat upright and started rolling up his pant legs. "People think we're separate from nature, but we're not. I think that's one beautiful thing the Luna pod has that we don't back home. They treat the ocean as if they're a part of it, rather than something to claim ownership of."

Noah stood and stepped into the calm waters, until the sea was at his knees. He twisted his hands, and tiny fish whose scales shimmered in the moonlight began to swirl around him as if dancing with him. Noah commanded a column of water to spiral upward, rising as tall as he was, then placed his fingers in the water to tickle the fish. They curiously nipped at his fingers. I watched closely, noticing how gentle he was with the marine life.

"These little guys don't care about our intentions, good or bad," Noah noted. "But the choices we make impact them, which in turn affects us. If we were to overfish or pollute these waters, they'd be gone along with our food source. To live a good life, you have to honor the life around you, rather than acting like you're separate or like there are things beneath you that you can shape and mold to your will, even if it's something like the ocean that can't consciously bite back."

"If you try to control the sea, you'll be sorely disappointed," I agreed. My fingers went to the sand, and I began tracing twisting lines through it reminiscent of ocean waves. "I think control is merely an illusion. You can overpower others if you're strong enough, but how much control do you truly have of the outcome? You can never control how other people feel, or how they'll react. You can't account for every variable nature throws at you. All you can really control is what *you* choose to do when you're faced with a decision."

"That's why I want to be intentional about what I choose to do with my future." Noah stepped out of the water and took a seat beside me on the blanket. "I know I can't plan for everything, but I can always make choices that reflect what kind of person I want to be, and I want to be someone who cares about the impact I'm making. If I were to open a restaurant, I think it could be more than that. I always pictured having a gift shop next door, something where we could utilize the waste from the restaurant and turn things like clam shells into art, or reuse it in some other sustainable way."

I glanced at the drawing I'd made in the sand, and I thought his idea of sustainable artwork sounded amazing. All forms of art were filled with stories that brought us closer together. To be able to express oneself and then share a piece of that self-expression with others seemed like the greatest honor in the world, and something I wanted to be a part of.

"That sounds... amazing," I told him.

"It does," he agreed. "I just... haven't figured out exactly what it will all look like yet. I think like Sal, I'd need a partner to make it all come together."

His gaze connected with mine, and I was suddenly aware of how close we were, so close that I could see the sparkle in his eye that said he meant more than he was willing to say aloud. Almost like he was talking about *me*.

His meaning barely registered before Noah was inching forward. At first, I thought he was going to kiss me, and I hesitated. But instead, he reached for a loose strand of hair that was blowing across my face and tucked it behind my ear. Noah noticed me stiffen and quickly yanked back, but the warmth of his touch lingered on my skin.

"Sorry," he rushed to say, which felt weird because when I was with Noah, we were never in a rush for anything. And when he touched me just now, I felt an immense sense of comfort wash over me.

I thought of everything we'd been through recently, and how easy it was to be open and vulnerable with him during our late-night chats. Noah seemed to understand me in a way no one else could, and his deep love for Sea Haven made me want to return home with him. We shared a common goal and wanted to restore magic to our home together. Noah and I made *sense*.

I realized then that I didn't want him to apologize, or to stop. I wanted to know what his arms would feel like around me, because with Noah, I felt safe.

"You don't have to apologize," I told him. "It's okay if you want to kiss me."

Noah's gaze dropped to my lips, his eyes twinkling with desire. "I *do* want to kiss you."

"Then what are you waiting for?" I whispered.

Time seemed to stop as Noah closed the distance between us. His lips brushed softly against mine, sending tingles dancing over my skin. Kissing Noah felt like the right thing to do, like one way or another we were always going to end up on a beach, the moonlight twinkling off the water and the scent of Sal's recipes wafting through the air.

But as he moved to deepen the kiss, nerves ignited in my stomach. I couldn't tell if that was good or bad.

Noah drew away, and I felt my stomach drop, but not because the kiss was over. This was... something else.

"I've wanted to do that for a long time," Noah admitted.

I wished to say something back, but the words wouldn't form on my tongue.

Noah noticed, and a worried crease formed between his brows. "How was it for you?"

I knew I could be honest with Noah, and that was the best thing about our friendship, but this felt... different. "To tell the truth, I don't know how I feel," I admitted.

Noah nodded understandingly, which made me really confused why I hesitated. I *wanted* to feel something more with him, because he was perfect in every way. I'd felt so conflicted earlier in the night, but then when Noah sat beside me on the beach and illuminated the sand beneath me, it felt like I was supposed to be there in his arms. The kiss was good, but it scared me that as much as I wanted him, something outside of my control was holding me back.

"We'll take things slow," he promised. "You just tell me if it's too much, all right?"

I nodded, though I already felt like I'd ruined the moment. "Would you just... hold me?"

"Of course." Noah moved closer and wrapped his arms around me.

We laid back on the blanket, and I relaxed into his embrace as I stared up at the stars. Noah was so warm, and the sound of his heartbeat soothed me. *This* felt natural. So why was I holding back?

I realized I'd always been told how to feel, never really questioning the emotions I suppressed. Now I was free to make up my own mind, and I didn't even know where to start, because I didn't know what my own feelings were telling me.

One thing I knew for certain, though, was that when I kissed Noah, my mind had been consumed with thoughts of someone else.

And being with that person was one choice that wasn't mine to make.

CHAPTER 18

Noah and I didn't speak about the kiss after it happened, but I asked him to stay with me that night because I didn't want to be alone. He agreed, but sleeping in the same bed felt too intimate. We weren't there yet, so Noah slept on the bench outside while I lay awake staring at the ceiling in the cabin. It was nice knowing he was there only a few steps away, because it felt like he could protect me from any harm. But at the same time, it felt wholly unfair to him. I knew nothing could ever happen between Tristan and me, but it wasn't fair to Noah to be my second choice.

I wanted to see Tristan again, only because I needed to

get rid of this desire I had for him. Tristan was engaged, and we came from different worlds. There was no future between us, and I wasn't going to let some fantasy of what could never happen ruin what could be a very real thing with Noah. All those things Noah had said on the beach were things I could see myself doing with him, and I *wanted* to explore where things could go with us—to follow that current to wherever my destiny led me.

I just had to get Tristan out of my head for good to do it.

Tristan and I were scheduled for training, and he'd asked me to meet him in the palace. One of the guards recognized me when I arrived.

"This way, Miss Waters." The guard led me through the palace corridors, until we came upon a long hall wider than any I'd seen in all of Luna City. At the end of the corridor was an expansive doorway, arched on the top and bottom and carved intricately with sculptures of shells and coral.

The guard gestured me through the doorway, before leaving to take his post again. I entered into a massive cavern with a high ceiling and beautiful columns that housed colorful coral. Tall windows had been carved out in the ceiling, and long benches stretched across the room, facing a raised stage. It was all grand and reminded me of a cathedral.

Tristan floated above the stage, his arms open wide and his smile bright and welcoming. My stomach flip-flopped when I saw him, which was the exact *opposite* of how I should feel around him. "Welcome to the Choral Sanctuary."

I kicked my scuba fins to spin through the water to take it all in. My skirt swirled around my legs, and my voice rang off the walls. "Tristan, this place is amazing!"

He swam down from the stage to come to my side. "This is where the Luna pod holds concerts and certain sacred ceremonies. The acoustics are excellent, which is why I thought we could try to coax out your siren song here."

"You... want me to sing?" I asked apprehensively. I thought of how I'd tried to sing with the pod at the fall equinox celebration, and how the melody caught in my throat. I doubted anything had changed overnight.

"You felt the song last night. I know you did. That feeling is still fresh, so let's see if we can turn it into something." Tristan placed a gentle hand on my back, nudging me toward the front of the room. "Go ahead and take center stage. Don't be shy—I'm the only one here."

I eyed him sideways. "That's not the encouragement you think it is."

Tristan laughed because he thought I was joking, but I wasn't. Still, I swam onto the stage, floating down through the water until my feet landed on the cavern floor. Sunlight filtered in through a hole in the ceiling, projecting down onto me like a spotlight. I lifted my hand to shield my eyes.

"To access your siren song, you have to feel the music in your bones," Tristan instructed. "Allow the melody to move through you, not just in your throat but your whole body."

I tried to open my mouth to sing something, but my teeth clamped together. Tristan made it sound so easy, and it *should* be, yet I found my heart racing and my hands growing clammy.

"I don't know what to sing," I admitted. "All the beautiful songs I've heard the Luna pod sing are in ancient languages I don't know."

"You don't need to use words," Tristan said. "Allow the melody to come through you."

"Okay, I'll try it," I agreed, though my voice squeaked as I began to move through several notes. I tried to recreate the melody I'd heard the pod sing at the enchanting ceremony, and my voice echoed off the tall ceiling.

Tristan's smile grew wider, his eyes sparkling up at me like he was entranced. Except he couldn't be, because my song fell flat, like I was choking out the tune. There were no ethereal notes of siren magic layered in as there should be.

My voice softened, the echo around the room fading to silence.

"You're doing great," Tristan encouraged. "Keep going."

I trembled as frustration rose within me. Standing up here—trying to perform for him—made it feel I was trying to be something I wasn't.

"I... I can't," I stammered.

Tristan's brows pinched together in worry. "What is it, Bree?"

I sagged to the corner of the stage, sitting so that my feet dangled off the edge. "Forcing my siren call is never going to work. I know the melody to the song, but I don't *feel* it. You say a siren song is about protection, but I don't know how to protect myself when I'm this scared, Tristan."

I didn't even realize I was frightened until I said it out loud.

He came to sit beside me, his beautiful fins curling out before him. "If that's the case, then let me protect you. If you never find your siren song, then so be it, because the rest of us will be there to raise our voices for you."

He spoke so soft and gentle, with almost a hint of a siren song coming through. I *wanted* to believe him, but I just... didn't.

"That would never be enough for me," I said honestly. "Knowing my powers are out there but just out of my reach is devastating. I found my voice with my sonic scream, but what good is it if I can't move people into action? The king still doesn't believe me about what I saw on that helicopter that day at the drillship, so how can I join in a choir of people who don't even know me? If I can't protect my people from my own council or the Luna pod from extermination, then I will never find my siren song because I can't even protect myself from my greatest fears."

"What are your greatest fears?" Tristan wondered.

My hands knotted in my lap. "I'm not sure I know. It's easy for you to feel like connection is enough because you know these people, but my sense of community has been shattered, and I don't know how long it will take to put the pieces back together. I thought my people had this big, beautiful community with the Sea Festival, but now it just feels like an illusion to try to convince us how close we were, when we couldn't give a damn about each other the rest of the year. Our magic should connect us, but we were robbed of it. So I learned how to stand up for myself, but never how to *connect* with myself. I don't even know who I am, and I'm not sure I ever did."

"I know who you are," he insisted. "You're confident, determined, and brave. You're the girl who will do anything to make things right, including traveling halfway across the country to get her magic back, then dodge bullets to break a stranger out of captivity. Where's the bold Bree I met back in Sea Haven?"

"She's gone, because she was never real in the first place." I jumped down from the stage, swaying my scuba fins to swim back and forth in front of him. "Maybe I don't want to be the girl who acts on impulse and has outbursts because she can't understand her own feelings. I never questioned who I was because, like my magic, I was never taught that I could be something more. Everything I've ever known is built off a lie. Now that I know there's more for me, I have to break down every piece of who I thought I was and rebuild it, hoping that there's a siren call or a mermaid tail hiding somewhere deep inside of me, but I haven't made any progress so I can't know if they're actually there or not."

"You're not alone," Tristan assured me. "Leaving home for the first time is scary, and you didn't get a chance to transition because you didn't get to make that choice for yourself. Sometimes growing up means you have to tear down the parts of yourself that were never you to begin with."

"How do I know what's me, and what's other people's expectations of me?" I demanded. "Ever since I came here, I can't make sense of who I am or how I feel. All I want to do is help, and I'm useless without my powers. I'm afraid I'll never be a real mermaid because I don't feel like one, and don't know *how* to be one."

"Is that what you're truly scared of?" Tristan asked gently.

"I'm scared of the truth, Tristan! The truth is, I can never return to Sea Haven the same knowing what I know, and I don't belong here either. Maybe the fact is that no matter how much I want to help clean up these messes, there's nothing I can actually do about it. I've put my trust in people who have broken it, and now I don't trust anyone anymore—not even myself, and not you."

Tristan reeled back, his demeanor quickly shifting. He was clearly offended. "Me?"

I couldn't stop the truth from tumbling out of my mouth. "All those things you said at the shipwreck sounded nice, but it's obvious you're hiding something behind those pretty words and half-truths. I've been lied to my whole life. I can't handle you lying to me too. I thought we could just be friends, but it's obvious you love Cordelia, so don't try to pretend to be something more than my mentor then leave me sitting alone. It's better if you just leave me alone altogether."

I went to turn away, but Tristan pushed himself off the stage, reaching out for my hand to stop me. He whirled me around, pulling me closer as frustration knitted in his brows.

"You want to know what I wished to say that day at the shipwreck—what I was desperately holding back?" Tristan demanded, like he couldn't stop himself. "The truth is when we're together, I can forget that I'm a prince who has to do everything a certain way all the time, and that includes marrying the girl my father chose for me. I take my duty to my people very seriously, but I don't think I should have to put on a charade to serve them."

I thought of the crown and the trident at the autumn equinox ceremony, and how he looked so different from the way I saw him—even sounded different than the close friend I'd come to know.

"When I'm with you, I don't have to play this prim and proper game and pretend to be something I'm not to get you to look up to me," he insisted. "You already see me for who I am, and it is *me* who looks up to *you*, as it should be. A prince should be inspired by his people. Since the day I met you, you have always spoken your mind, and I wish to do the same."

My skin tingled from where he touched it, and my breath wavered. I wanted to run, because dodging his words like bullets felt like the easier thing to do. But there was a deeper part of me that desired to know his every truth. "Then tell me, what are you afraid to say?"

"I'm afraid to tell my father that I wish to be an explorer," Tristan said. "I've remained hidden behind our protection spell my whole life, but I should be the one protecting others now. There's a reason I volunteered to organize an expedition to Sea Haven—because I wanted to learn from the rest of the world and bring that knowledge back to my people, like my mother did. That's how I believe I'll serve them best, not by sitting on a throne following the same script as every king before me. That worked for my father, and his arranged marriage with my mother was beautiful, but that's not what I want for myself. I'm afraid to break the order of things, because I don't want to put the Luna pod at risk, or without a leader as I was trained to be."

Tristan lifted a hand to the side of my face, his blue-green eyes sparkling down at me. "I love being a prince, but I want to be a king in my own way. Ever since I met you, Bree, all I've wanted was to forgo the traditions of old and carve my own path. If a king and queen must work together, then I must decide for myself who I want at my side. I won't accept a centuries-old tradition that pairs me with someone whom I don't wish to be with. The truth is, I didn't mention my engagement to Cordelia because she means nothing to me. I don't want her. I want *you*."

Tristan took my face in both hands, swooping his lips down until they were a mere inch from my own. He hesitated, and I didn't need to hear it out loud to comprehend the full admission of how he felt. He was awaiting my approval, and if I was being entirely honest with myself, I didn't want to miss this chance with him.

I barely had to think about it. A split second passed before I lifted my chin and our lips connected. All the saltwater left my lungs as my breath hitched, that school of fish in my belly going wild as he dragged me even closer. My heart lifted, feeling lighter than air, as if his kiss could lift me all the way to the surface.

His arms curled around me, pulling me into a deep embrace. We lifted away from the ocean floor and went spiraling upward, high above the stage. My lips parted, and Tristan's tongue danced over mine, sending my heart crashing against my chest like ocean waves against a cliffside—

A cliffside I'd just tumbled over, freefalling into waters that might either break my fall... or drown me completely.

I drew away from him, gasping desperately for the breath he'd stolen. My lips still tingled from his kiss.

Tristan lifted his hand, unfurling his fingers between us. In his palm sat a perfect pearl, the one I thought he'd tossed into the whirlpool last night.

"You never finished your ceremony," I remarked.

He shook his head. "I tried to, but I couldn't. I knew my father might need me, and I wasn't ready to make any mistakes. But I am now. If you are a mistake, then so be it, because you're all I want."

Tristan leaned down to pull me into another kiss, but I yanked away. All I heard was his voice echoing the word *mistake* over and over in my mind. And I just couldn't face the possibility that that's what this was—a horrible mistake that, like all my others, would blow up in my face.

Tristan didn't say it out loud, but I knew the implications of what this meant. Being with him meant becoming a queen to a pod that wasn't my own. I didn't belong among them, and I certainly couldn't fill the role as their queen. It was the queen's job to make choices for her people, and I couldn't even make up my mind for myself. Tristan was all but asking me to take the fate of his people in my hands.

"I—I'm sorry," I stammered. "We shouldn't do this."

I turned and fled, my head reeling as I commanded a current to rise up and push me out of the room. I left Tristan floating there in the middle of the room without so much as a proper explanation.

I couldn't even explain it to myself. All I'd wanted was the truth...

Only to find the truth was far more terrifying than the lie.

CHAPTER 19

I raced back toward the palace entrance, the water propelling me forward like a jet stream. The hallways seemed like they were closing in on me, like I had to get to the surface before I ran out of air.

I rounded a corner and ran into someone. We both gave a heavy *oof*, as we tumbled backward through the water. When I righted myself, I saw that I'd run into Liana.

"Bree!" my best friend cried. "Are you okay?"

Oxygen seemed to return to my lungs, but I still hesitated. "I don't think so."

Her features fell. Never in my life had I told Liana I

wasn't okay, so she knew it must be bad. "Let's go to my room and talk," she offered.

There was nothing I wanted more than to be with her to clear my head.

Liana led me down a few twisting corridors until we came upon a round door made of a giant scallop shell that hinged at the bottom, opening up like a clam. We entered the room, and the door shut softly behind us.

Liana's quarters were grand, with a high ceiling and a circular seashell bed lined with silky aqua-colored seaweed sheets. A tall window took up nearly the entirety of one wall, which had thin draping curtains to provide privacy. The room glowed a bluish hue that seemed to dance with the shifting water and flow with the movement of the fish outside.

"Sit down and tell me all about it," Liana ordered, pointing to a luxurious vanity with a shimmering shell mirror.

I sank into the chair, and Liana began to brush out my hair, sectioning it off for French braids like we used to do at our sleepovers back home.

"I kissed Tristan," I admitted.

She gasped, her jaw dropping dramatically. "For real?"

I nodded, my cheeks flushing. "And Noah."

In the reflection of the mirror, I watched her jaw drop further. "Ooh," she practically sang. "Tell me more."

Liana acted almost silly about it, which helped me ease into the story. It was easy to talk to her, like we were back home in her bedroom when we used to debate about fictional boys.

I told her all about what happened last night with Noah, and how I'd pulled away from him even though I wanted the kiss to happen. Then I recounted this morning with Tristan, and how I'd gotten so frustrated about my powers and snapped. I told her all about Tristan's confession, and how I hadn't stopped him when he swooped in to kiss me—how I'd even *wanted* it.

She secured my braids, and I dropped my face into my hands. "I don't understand how I can want them both at once. I've never felt so conflicted."

Liana sat on the bed. "Our lives changed abruptly. I don't blame you for being confused."

I turned around in my chair, leaning over the back to face her. "Which makes worrying about boys right now really stupid. Tristan was right, Liana. I used to punch back, and now I feel like I'm hurting myself just to prove how much I can take. Am I taking this all too seriously?"

"No," she assured me. "You've been through a lot. Not only was your magic taken and you had to fight to get it back, but we were forced to leave our families with no way to contact them, and we'd be risking our lives if we returned alone."

"At least my dad knows we're alive and can assume we're in good hands. I'm sure he's told your parents."

"Which has brought me a lot of comfort since arriving here," Liana said. "But that's beside the point. I think Noah and Tristan both mean a lot to you, and pretending like you can compartmentalize your feelings until this is all over isn't going to help anything. You're taking these guys seriously because you *are* serious about them."

"I guess you're right." I stood, absentmindedly straightening up the vanity to give myself something to do. "Noah's like an anchor for me. He can calm me down just by being near me, and I can open up to him and talk about deep stuff. We connect over things from back home, and he makes me want to remember the good things, when I could so easily become bitter over a childhood that's now tainted by lies. With Noah, there's this hope that our home isn't gone, nor a complete lie, but something we can make better by expanding on all the good it has to offer. And I *want* to do that with him, but I can't decide if I want to do it as his friend... or as his girlfriend."

"And Tristan?" Liana wondered.

I straightened the brush on the vanity. "I've learned a lot from him, not just how to connect with the ocean and summon a storm, but I see how he connects with his people, and that's so beautiful. But... I never know what he's really thinking. Sometimes it's so simple that I can't tell if there's more underneath the surface. My feelings for Tristan feel electric, but chaotic. Besides, he's engaged to Cordelia, and even if he broke that off, he still pursued me while he was engaged. That's not okay."

Liana shrugged. "It sounds like he never wanted the engagement in the first place. It's a gray area."

"Maybe you're right," I said. "Noah's safe and makes me feel at home, but Tristan's like this big adventure I want to be a part of. Tristan pushes me to do better, but with Noah I can be vulnerable and he teaches me more about who I am. I need them both."

Liana wiggled her eyebrows playfully. "So date them both."

I slumped to the bed beside her. "That may work for some people, but not for me. When I make a decision, I stick with it, and I don't want to make the wrong choice."

"You just have to trust your instincts," she encouraged. "I know you'll make the choice that's right for you."

A high-pitched shriek came from outside the palace, cutting our conversation off. It was so loud that it shook the palace walls, as if someone was using their supersonic scream to send an alarm signal across all of Luna City.

Liana and I exchanged a startled look, both unsure of what was happening. Then commotion came from down the hall as guards' voices overlapped one another. We rushed over to the window to see what was going on, and what I saw caused all the saltwater to leave my lungs.

From our vantage point in the palace, we could see far out over the city. A dark, murky cloud streaked through the water, leading from the surface all the way down to the seafloor. We couldn't make out what was happening on the ocean bottom past the seamounts that made up most of the city, but I could see guards hurrying out of the palace entrance and gathering near the Bar. I peered closer at the cloudy substance billowing like smoke, and noticed it contained a reddish hue.

My stomach lurched when I realized what it was.

Blood.

And a lot of it.

Liana gasped and clutched her chest as she took in the horrifying scene. "Oh, my god!"

I sprang into action immediately, whirling around and into the hall, where Lamar was swimming by with a spear in his hand. Liana hesitated, then followed behind me.

"Lamar," I called. "What's happening?"

"There's been an attack. Please, ladies, stay in your room where it's safe." Lamar turned away from us and flicked his fins, disappearing around the corner a second later.

Liana and I exchanged a glance. My intentions must've been written across my face, because her eyes widened. "Bree, no! You're not following the guards to the Bar. We don't know what's going on out there. It could be dangerous!"

"Which is exactly why we can't sit around doing nothing," I insisted. "We have to help."

Liana grabbed my wrist to stop me. "Why do *you* have to be the one to save everyone?"

"Because the Luna pod came to *us* for help. I won't walk away from them."

"You stumbled upon them by chance," Liana pressed. "Do you really think they came to Sea Haven looking for *teenagers* to help save their dying ecosystem? We don't have any military or medical experience, or relevant training of any kind that's actually useful in the field. You don't even have access to your full powers, so what are you going to do? We are the last people who should be out there responding to threats. You could get hurt!"

I sank several inches through the water. Liana wasn't being mean; she was only concerned for my safety, and I couldn't blame her. We'd been thrown into all of this all because I happened to be out for a midnight walk and stumbled upon something I shouldn't have. We hadn't been chosen because we had some unique advantage that could bring all this conflict to an end. I just happened to be in the wrong place at the wrong time.

Intentional or not, though, we were a part of this now, and I could either see it through or run away. That decision wasn't even a question for me.

"You're right," I told Liana. "I'm not as strong or capable—or even as magical—as everyone else here. I don't have the knowledge, training, or resources to save these people, and offering my help may not actually change the outcome. But I know if I go back into that room to cower away, I'll never stop regretting that decision. Maybe the choices I'm afraid to make aren't singular, massive decisions that will change the course of the future for everyone. Maybe they're small choices in every moment that will add up to something bigger years from now. Those smaller choices start here. If you want to stay here where it's safe, then I won't stop you, but I'm going out there and helping wherever I can."

A loud, mournful wail reverberated off the palace walls from somewhere far in the distance. Liana gave a shudder, like she couldn't stand the thought of someone out there suffering.

Something changed in her then. She straightened her spine and wore an expression of bravery. "I'm not staying behind," she said firmly. "I'm coming with you."

I grabbed her hand. "Then there's no time to waste. Let's go."

CHAPTER 20

Liana and I rushed out of the palace. The Bar wasn't far from the entrance, and we could see a large crowd forming in the waters above the seafloor. I immediately noticed Tristan, who was floating high above the Bar beside Cordelia. He clutched the aquamarine stone around his neck, appearing horrified. We made our way over to them, until we'd climbed high enough over the rocks that we could see the scene below. My stomach dropped as we came to a halt.

Below us, a baby humpback whale lay bleeding in the sand with a harpoon sticking out of its side. The mother was beside her daughter, letting out a cry of desperation that rocked the whole city. I recalled seeing these whales swimming overhead when Tristan brought me to the Landing. Their song had sounded so beautiful then, but now the notes shattered my heart.

Sanvi sat in the sand, running her hands over the baby whale's head to help soothe her, while she ordered other merfolk to bring healing herbs as quickly as possible. Blood continued to pour out of the deep wound, staining the water a deep red. I feared they didn't have the time to save the whale.

Cordelia's gaze snapped in my direction, and her lips curled back in disgust. She flicked her purple fins, until she was right in front of me. "You tell us how to fix this!" she snarled cruelly.

"I—I don't know," I stammered, reeling back.

"You're supposed to be here to *help* us," she sneered. "You've lived on the surface all your life, so don't tell me you don't understand these weapons and how to combat them."

"I'm not a harpoon specialist," I snapped.

"Give us *something*," Cordelia begged.

"What do you expect us to do?" Liana growled, coming to my defense.

Tristan shoved himself between us. "Stop it, Cordelia. This is not Bree's fault, and you know it."

"Whether it's her fault or not, the surface-dwellers have escalated," Cordelia demanded. "An attack on our wildlife is an attack on us. If Bree had given us something useful, we could've driven them away by now. They won't get away with this!"

"No, we won't let them," Tristan agreed. "My father should be here any moment. We must await his orders."

"So he can tell us to bide our time?" Cordelia scoffed. "I'm done waiting."

She whirled around, leaving a trail of bubbles behind her as she raced back into the city.

"Cordelia, wait," Tristan demanded, but she didn't listen. His teeth gritted. "For the Kraken's sake."

He took off behind her, and Liana and I followed as fast as we could, maneuvering through twists and turns between seamounts. I nearly lost track of Tristan, before coming upon The Marina.

When Liana and I entered Cordelia's shop, there were already other merfolk there. Cordelia was passing out spears, tridents, daggers, and shields to groups of men and women who were shaking with rage from what they'd seen at the Bar.

"This is not the way!" Tristan bellowed.

Cordelia's features darkened. "What are you going to do? Tell these people *not* to fight? If that's the case, then what have we been training for all this time? Our time to fight is now!"

"Yes, but not without the king's orders," Tristan insisted. "We have to do this right. These spears and blades are archaic compared to the weapons these people have. Our weapons only work if we are strategic about it, and so we have to do this together, or it will be chaos. You go against the king, and you will get us all killed. We cannot rush in without a plan!"

Cordelia grabbed two spears, one with a purple tip that matched her fins, and another with a green spearhead. "I plan to kill them all."

"My parents' division cost us greatly the last time, and if you do this, you're risking the same outcome as before," Tristan demanded.

"*Someone* needs to make this call! Your father is too afraid to make this decision, and so are you. I'm going to be queen soon, and it's time I start acting like it."

Tristan shook his head and backed away from her. "No, you won't be, because this engagement is over."

My whole body stilled in shock, and Liana's jaw dropped from beside me.

Cordelia scoffed. "Good, because I don't want to be with someone who can't protect his people when it comes down to it. At least one of us will go down in history having done the right thing—"

A massive explosion shook the entire city, causing rocks to tumble from the cave ceiling overhead. People screamed and ducked for cover, and Liana and I grabbed each other, crouching to avoid falling debris. Panicked cries echoed throughout the city.

Tristan's features paled, and he raced past me out the door to see what was going on. The rest of us followed. As we swam upward out of the crevices in the rock, we could see far across the city, where a cloud of dirt swelled upward at least a hundred feet. The echo of rocks tumbling over one another reached our ears, and the shimmer of mertails glistened in the distance as seafolk fled.

We couldn't tell how many people had been hurt by the blast, but I noticed the detonation had occurred near the edge of the city, where very few merfolk resided. It almost seemed intentional... like a warning rather than a direct attack.

"What is this?" Cordelia hissed. "Some sort of volcanic activity?"

One could only hope... but no. Far off in the distance, in the direction of the drill site, a dark spot moved across the surface of the water. It looked so small from this far away, but I knew the threat was far larger than it appeared.

"It's... a missile," I stated breathlessly. "I don't understand. The drillship is a civilian vessel. They shouldn't have all these weapons aboard."

"Obviously they're here for more than just their oil," Cordelia sneered.

My stomach churned as I watched the dot on the surface move closer, growing larger with each passing second.

Tristan shook his head in confusion. "How is this possible? They're too close to the city. Our spell is stronger than ever. They should be compelled away by our enchantment."

"Unless they found a way around it," I stated hollowly, my hands clenching into fists.

Cordelia whirled toward Tristan. "You see what I mean? Your father has been wrecked by the queen's passing and has been too afraid to finish this in fear of someone else getting hurt, and that's a short-sighted way of thinking. The fact is, people are going to get hurt one way or another, but if the king continues to sit around on his fins, we will *all* perish. I'm willing to risk my life so that others may live. What are you willing to give up?"

"You think I'm unwilling to risk it all?" Tristan demanded. "I've lost my mother and five of my closest friends. I will give up everything for my people, but if we can't do this together then we have nothing!"

"Then prove it." Cordelia shoved the green spear into his hand, then moved past him and called over the city. "This has gone on far too long, and we are now out of time. If these surface-dwellers want a fight, we'll give them one. Who's with me!?"

Hundreds of merfolk emerged from the sea caves, clutching their spears and tridents.

Maren was the first to swim forward, her silver scales gleaming like armor. "I have sworn a duty to protect our people. I will sink their ship before I allow them to take this city. Let's make them pay for the lives they've taken, so that they can take no others!"

"Make them pay!" a merman echoed.

All around us, seafolk rose upward with a battle cry. Cordelia lifted her purple spear overhead, and my stomach twisted. This couldn't end well.

"What is the meaning of this?" a deep voice demanded.

We turned to see King Aalto had approached, flanked

by at least fifty guards. I noticed Noah and Lamar among them. Noah rushed to my side, but we didn't have a chance to exchange words before Cordelia was answering the king.

"That ship is too close to the city!" she cried. "We're fighting, with or without your orders."

King Aalto reeled back, blinking in shock. I didn't think anyone had ever defied his orders before. His gaze traveled out over the city, toward the site of the blast, and his features fell hopelessly. It was heartbreaking to watch, honestly. Tristan had said they were running out of time, and now the king had to face the reality that he hadn't moved quick enough to save everyone.

King Aalto's gaze dropped to the trident in his hand. "If that is the way the Luna pod feels, then I'm afraid I haven't lived up to my duties as your reigning monarch."

"Father, you can't back down now!" Tristan insisted. "If we stand any chance of surviving the day, we must do so united."

"You are correct, son." King Aalto turned toward the crowd, raising his voice. "I have spent so long clinging to my failures of the past, desperate to prevent them from occurring again. You deserve a king who will not let the weight of his lowest moments crush him and cause him to retreat. You need a leader who can adapt to changing tides, who holds on to hope when all seems lost. I will not allow history to repeat itself. This time *will* be different, because I will not be leading you in this fight."

Gasps traveled around the crowd.

King Aalto removed the silver crown atop his head and presented it to Tristan. "My son, I have hesitated giving up this crown, claiming you weren't ready for it. In reality, it was *I* who was not ready to give up my role in protecting you. I sent you to Sea Haven because I believed it would be a safe journey, but I cannot continue to pretend as if I can control the outcome of each order I give. You have proven yourself more than capable of exploring possibilities without the need for certainty to face it. Even at your rock bottom, you express gratitude and step in when others need support. Will you accept your birthright as king, to lead these people into this battle with the tenacity and strength you have shown me time and time again that you possess?"

Hesitation crossed Tristan's features. King Aalto didn't want to fight, and in my opinion he was being a coward for giving up his position this close to losing it all. If the Luna pod perished today, then at the very least that blood wasn't on his hands.

But I also didn't think King Aalto had what it took to make difficult decisions and lead these people in this fight. If he had to step down so Tristan could take over, then so be it. Tristan would make a better king anyway.

In Tristan's moment of hesitation, I swam forward and placed my hand in his. "You said you wanted to do right by your people. Right now, the Luna pod needs you more than ever."

Tristan gazed down at me. "A great leader needs a partner, and I have no queen beside me."

"You don't need one," I told him. "You said you wanted to be a king in your own way. Now's your chance."

Tristan squeezed my hand tightly. "You're right. I *can* do this my way."

Tristan dropped my hand and turned toward the king. The uncertainty faded from his expression, replaced with stone cold resolve. "I accept, Father."

Then King Aalto placed the crown atop Tristan's head, and the prince threw back his shoulders, turning to the crowd now as their king.

Seeing Tristan in that crown gave me chills. It seemed to cause a piece of himself to emerge, one wholly confident in what needed to be done. It didn't surprise me one bit that he immediately embodied the role of a king, because he already possessed all the qualities of a great leader.

"We will fight, but we must do it *together*," Tristan stated firmly. He turned toward the guards, pointing to a dozen merfolk, including Noah. "You get these people to safety in the deepest of sea caves near the Ancestral Trench. The rest of you are with me! We attack from all angles and take their men down with the ship."

His father nodded. "You heard the king!"

Aalto followed Tristan as merfolk began to disperse in separate directions.

I turned to go with them, but Noah grabbed my arm to stop me. "It's not safe for you up there. Come with me to help the guards round up civilians."

"I can't," I told him, my mind already made up. "I may not have my mermaid tail or my siren call, but I can brew one hell of a storm, and right now I have to be on the surface where I can put my powers to good use."

Noah didn't argue with me, or try to convince me it was too dangerous. Instead, he pulled me into a tight embrace and whispered, "Stay safe."

I squeezed him back, then drew away to look him in the eyes. "When I was exiled from Sea Haven, you brought me home, Noah. Now you have to make sure these people get to come home, too. I'll be up there on the surface making sure they have a home to come back to."

Noah nodded firmly in agreement. "You come back, too, all right?"

I lifted my little finger. "I pinky promise."

He looped his finger through mine. "Promise."

Then we turned and went our separate ways, diving head-first into a fight that would either save the seafolk...

Or kill us all.

CHAPTER 21

My heart hammered, but the thought to turn back never crossed my mind. I kicked my scuba fins, sprinting to catch up with the merfolk who were already far ahead of me. I commanded a current to rise up and carry me forward, until I swam up between Tristan and Liana.

Tristan glanced my way. "Are you sure this is the path you wish to follow?"

"It's not a question," I told him. "You said we could save our homes together. Let's go save yours."

We neared the surface, and already merfolk were summoning deadly powers that rocked the incoming ship from side to side. Huge waves rose up to crash into the hull of a massive metal seacraft. It was different from the drillship, as this one was all gray and looked like something used by the military, though there were no notable markings to indicate which military it belonged to. However the humans got their hands on this ship, it proved to be as deadly as any other military vessel. Another missile blasted out of the ship's underbelly, exploding against the outskirts of the city and causing multiple sea caves to crumble in moments.

Sonic screams echoed across the ocean, igniting a burning rage within me. I didn't know how this ship, and the people operating it, made it past the Luna pod's enchantment, but they weren't getting any closer to this city if I had anything to say about it.

I lifted my hands toward the surface, allowing my fury to unleash. The ocean connected with me, her raging currents becoming one with my anger. Water churned, and the sunlight that had been shining down on the city just this morning was completely blocked out by a thick layer of clouds that seemed to transform the day to night in seconds. My fury mixed with the magic of other merfolk whose rage had ignited a tempest. Lightning flashed, and thunder rocked the skies as the merfolk broke the surface of the water, collectively poised for attack.

Not a second was wasted. Tristan commanded a waterspout to carry him upward, and he went spiraling toward the deck of the ship, his spear aimed for impact as a sonic scream ripped from his lungs. Hundreds of merfolk followed, their voices overlapping one another as their screams shook the entire boat.

I held back, allowing the waves to rock me from side to side as I danced with the ocean and called her storm to the surface. A torrential downpour burst from the clouds, and the waves swelled higher.

At least a hundred men in black clothing were already waiting aboard the enemy ship with their weapons ready. They opened fire, but the merfolk's collective screams caused the ship to rock and the men to lose their aim. Gunfire rang out, and bullets hit the cresting waves.

Merfolk and humans alike were caught in the crossfire within moments, and blood spilled across the deck.

I witnessed Tristan's spear sink into a man's gut, and he wrenched it out, the tip stained red. He moved on to the next man, knocking the gun from his hand before commanding a waterspout to encase his entire head. The man gave a gurgle as he inhaled the water.

Cordelia did the same as Tristan, spinning through a water column as if it were the tentacle of a large sea beast. Her spear pierced through several men's chests, before one of them shot a bullet in her direction, and it snapped her spear clean in half. She tossed the remaining bits aside, then reached out with her bare hands to yank the man downward and into the sea. She disappeared below the surface, dragging him to depths he couldn't survive, before she was back to do the same to others.

Aalto worked with a group of unarmed seafolk nearby to summon large waves that crashed over the boat and made the men in black either lose their footing or their weapons. At least a dozen men were caught up in the wave and fell off the deck into the churning waters below. Next to them, a large group of mermaids used their siren call to compel several men to jump ship.

Not far from me, Liana lifted her hands and called sea life to the surface. Octopuses, crabs, and other sea creatures responded to Liana's call for assistance, and they swarmed the deck. The enemy men became distracted and turned their gunfire on the creatures. Dolphins followed her instructions and leapt out of cresting ocean waves to land on the deck of the ship. They used their heavy tailfins to smack men in the face, knocking them down and disorienting them. I witnessed Maren following behind the dolphins, leaping from one waterspout to another and piercing men with her spear.

One of the men locked their aim on Liana, and my heart jumped.

"Liana!" I screamed, but he'd already opened fire.

Liana ducked into the water, and the bullets whizzed past her. She resurfaced, and her features darkened, her vengeful gaze set on the enemy men. A sonic scream erupted from her lungs, and the shockwave knocked the gun out of the man's hand. I joined in on the scream, and our voices resonated with one another to create a supersonic wave of power that hit him head-on. He threw his hands over his ears and fell to his knees as blood seeped between his fingers.

Even after all of that, we'd only managed to take out a

third of their men. Bullets continued to fly everywhere, and merfolk blood spilled into the water. We couldn't take much more of this without being forced to retreat, and if we did that, the city would be lost.

Aalto went pale as he took in the bloodshed. It'd all happened so fast.

Not far from me, Tristan readied for another attack. Aalto swam up to him and grabbed his arm. "Tristan, we aren't equipped to handle this! You must order our people to withdraw."

"No," Tristan demanded over the roar of the storm. "We will finish this!"

"Your mother would order the retreat!" Aalto cried.

"Queen Lorelei is not here," Tristan shot back. "You trusted me to lead our people into battle. If we leave now, the enemy will only return, and we will not survive another fight. Our only option is to capsize this ship and devastate the enemy forces until we gain the upper hand."

Aalto peered around at the fallen bodies. "I didn't think you'd take it this far!"

Tristan ripped his arm out of his father's grasp, glaring at him with disgust. "I can't believe you. You were too spineless to save my mother, and you're too spineless to save these people now!"

Tristan turned away, projecting his voice for all merfolk to hear. "Keep going!"

Aalto's eyes widened in horror. "No. We must retreat!"

Merfolk hesitated, and I feared Aalto was wrong. He thought he could correct his mistake from last time by making the same choice Queen Lorelei had, but these circumstances were different, and he was only repeating his mistake by dividing the pod.

The moment of indecision caused the men aboard the ship to regain their aim, putting their sights on the royals.

"Save the king!" someone cried.

Everything happened in the blink of an eye. Lamar threw himself in front of Tristan the same moment several gunshots rang across the skies. I flinched, and my heart lurched in terror. Bullets whizzed through the air and sliced through the water.

Aalto remained unguarded. He gave a sea-shuddering scream as bullet wounds ripped through his chest. My stomach clenched as I witnessed blood spurt from his wounds, staining the waters red. Aalto's screams turned to gurgles, and he sagged forward as the life drained from his eyes.

"Father, no!" Tristan wailed, leaping forward.

My heart shattered for him, for the former king, for the pod... for everyone who had lost someone dear to them today. We'd come here to defend this city, and it seemed that in no time at all, the enemy had left us completely devastated.

Tristan ducked underwater to go after his father, whose body was already drifting downward into the sea. I rushed to follow and saw that I wasn't the only one. Cordelia was also swimming in his direction, and Lamar had grabbed Tristan to stop him.

"It's too late, my king," Lamar said.

Tristan's features had gone completely blank. He glanced around at the carnage, like he couldn't believe what he was seeing. Bullets continued to slice through the water, and merfolk screams echoed against the seabed. Tristan remained frozen in indecision.

"What are we to do, King Tristan?" Lamar pressed.

Cordelia reached Tristan before I did. She grabbed him by the shoulders and shook him. "Forget your father, Tristan. You have to pull yourself together!"

She failed to rouse a response from him. Waves raged around us, yanking me from side to side. It took everything in me to fight the current and swim over to him. I was panting by the time I arrived.

Cordelia scoffed at me. "You really think he's going to listen to *you*?"

I shoved her out of the way, then took his hands to focus his attention on me. "Tristan, you have to give the order again."

His gaze snapped in my direction. "I—I don't know what order to give."

"You wanted to finish this, so we finish it," I told him. "Remember what you told me about what merfolk do when times get tough? We transmute the energy, and we turn it into something better. We can let your father's death stop us, or we can use it to push us onward."

Tristan swallowed. "You're right. I will not let my father's death be in vain."

Then his features transformed. He put on that strong, confident expression I knew him for.

"Put everything you have into this storm!" Tristan ordered the merfolk. "We're taking that ship down!"

We returned to the surface, where Liana, Maren, and Lamar gathered around us, along with at least a hundred other merfolk. Power came from all directions and swelled upward. Waves grew taller until they towered higher than buildings overhead. We had to work together and time this just right.

We worked with the rhythm of the ocean, allowing our outrage to fuel her tumultuous storm. The waves carried us higher and higher, until we crested a hundred feet above the rest of the sea, prepared to crash down on the enemy ship and bring her down with us.

Movement caught my eye, and from my vantage point atop the climbing wave, I witnessed a man with a briefcase step out of the seacraft's shadows. In the chaos, he was barely noticeable, but the means in which he casually strolled forward, like he was going for a walk along the beach, stole all of my attention. He moved as if he was completely unbothered by his surroundings, like the death toll didn't matter. He wore a suit, which made him look completely out of place. Lightning flashed and reflected off his bald head.

The blood in my veins turned to ice. It couldn't be...

I'd turn to stone, struck with horror as I watched a man I was certain was a ghost stroll to the center of the ship deck. He placed the briefcase at his feet, then bent to click it open.

"Watch out!" I tried to warn the others, but it was already too late.

I wasn't sure what to expect, but when the case sprang open, my worst fears were realized. From the briefcase, the man withdrew an amber-colored stone the size of his fist. It seemed to emit a dull light that flickered as if a fire were trapped inside the rock.

Everything shifted in a heartbeat. Power leeched out of me, and every ounce of magic that had been connected to the storm left my body. My throat closed up around a sonic scream that never came, and the marine life around me seemed more distant than ever.

The wave we'd been riding went crashing downward like someone else had stolen control, and my stomach bottomed out as I tumbled down with it. Thunder continued to rumble overhead, but the supersonic screams of my fellow merfolk were instantly silenced. All around me, the shimmering scales of merfolk tails dulled, and their beautiful fins morphed into legs against their will, their modesty protected by seaweed clothing. All at once, it was like their magic had been sucked out of them.

The stone in the man's hand grew brighter, illuminating his features until I could make out the raw scars across his neck. Victorious laughter broke out of his chest, making me want to hurl.

He lifted his hands, and streams of water blasted out of the sea, knocking spears and tridents from the merfolk's grasp. Waterspouts rose up all around us, swirling beneath each member of the Luna pod and lifting them into the air simultaneously. The man brought his hands down, sending a hundred of us slamming onto the deck of the ship all at once. Pain radiated throughout my entire body, but I managed to lift my head.

Merfolk screamed and scrambled backward, but the men aboard the ship were already waiting with a large net. They tossed the net over most of the merfolk so they couldn't escape, while the rest of us were left lying there, heaving for breath that had been knocked out of us when we crashed to the ship deck. Liana gave a pained groan beside me, and I caught sight of Cordelia in the net. She tried to rip through it with her bare hands, but the net was made of metal chains, and her efforts were in vain.

Several men took advantage of our disoriented state and grabbed Tristan. He was the only one whose scales were still shimmering against the lightning strikes. They dragged the merman across the deck as his tail thrashed, and secured zip ties around his wrists. Tristan tried to summon a massive wave, but he was cut off by a loud *bang* from a bullet someone had shot into the sky. It was a deadly warning.

The men reached down to rip the aquamarine stone from Tristan's neck. His scales disappeared, and his fins split in two to become legs.

Tristan appeared powerless on his knees, but he lifted his head high and spat, "We will not give up so easily!"

That earned him the butt of a pistol to the side of his head, and my heartbeat faltered at the sound of the impact.

Mere seconds had passed. Heavy footsteps approached

me, and I trembled as his shined shoes crossed the deck in my direction. I feared looking upward, for I knew I'd find the truth I didn't want to admit staring back at me.

The man holding the amber stone stopped in front of me, his familiar voice mocking. "What do we have here? Miss Waters, the girl who just can't stop causing me trouble."

Shaking, I lifted my gaze to peer into the eyes of the man I hated most in the world—a man I believed to be rotting in the belly of sharks.

Sea Haven council head Carson Ray.

CHAPTER 22

My gaze roamed over the red scars on Carson's neck that hadn't fully healed. The scars were new, but every other sick feature on his vile face was exactly as I remembered, though that desire for power that blazed behind his eyes had only grown more intense.

My arms shook as I tried to push myself upright, but Carson summoned another wave out of the ocean and slammed it into my back. My head cracked against the ship deck, making the world spin around me. I wished to fight back, but the strength I'd found while living with the Luna pod was absent. With the stone in his hand, Carson had reduced me to a former version of myself, with nothing more than the power to breathe underwater and control a few water droplets. The girl I was not so long ago felt so distant now; this weakness seemed unfamiliar.

"You're looking... *good*," I snarled. I eyed him closely because I knew he must have an aquamarine stone on him somewhere, but there wasn't anything around his neck. He must've learned from last time and concealed it better.

Carson scoffed. "I have you to thank for that. And the fact that you were too cowardly to finish the job yourself. You really thought I couldn't fight off a few sharks?"

"I'm sure you're used to swimming with them, considering you're a shark yourself—greedy and predatory," I sneered.

Carson's features spread into a twisted smile. "You say that like it's a bad thing, but sharks are also ruthless, and they always get what they want."

My gaze fell upon the amber-colored stone he held, and my insides revolted. "So that's your sea stone?"

"One of them," Carson stated proudly.

"That's how you got this ship past the pod's enchantment," I accused.

"Obviously," he said. "When will you realize, Miss Waters, that you are not as clever as you think? You just happen to show up in the wrong places at the wrong time."

"Like that day I was at the drill site," I spat. "That was you on that helicopter, wasn't it?"

Carson ignored my accusation. Instead, he kicked my scuba fins and laughed. "Cute. Looks like you never really gave up who I taught you to be. Don't forget who's really in power here, Miss Waters."

"So kill me already."

"I'm not here to kill you," he replied. "I'm here to use you. There's no use in letting your power—no matter how *pathetic*—go to waste when it benefits me so greatly."

Carson cocked his head, and two men rushed toward me. One of them secured a zip tie around my wrists in front of me, then they dragged me forward until I was forced to sit beside Tristan.

Carson began pacing in front of us. "This will be a lot easier if you all stop struggling."

"We deserve answers," Tristan demanded. "Bree asked you a question. Are you going to answer it, or shy away like a coward?"

Carson scoffed, staring down his nose at Tristan. "Ah, Prince Tristan Adamaris. I've already held you prisoner once. This time, I'll make sure you won't escape."

He yanked the silver crown off Tristan's head and tossed it to the side. It skidded across the deck and fell into the water. "There will be no point in using your royal title any longer. Not that you're deserving of it, anyway. You're so daft you can't figure out the truth without me spelling it out for you. Of *course* it was me that day on the helicopter."

"And yet you ran away," Tristan accused. "You

couldn't even show your face. My brother was looking for you. Is that what scared you off?"

Carson threw his head back, letting out a deep belly laugh that caught me off guard. "Zale? Scare *me*? Oh, dear prince. I'm afraid you have it all wrong. Zale and I have been working *together*."

My stomach dropped, and Tristan's features fell into an expression of disbelief. Cries of protest rose up among the merfolk.

"You're lying!" Tristan bellowed. "My brother would never!"

Footsteps sounded on the deck, and a shadow emerged from behind Carson. All eyes turned to see Prince Zale approaching.

"Surprised, brother?" Zale asked cruelly. "While you were all sitting around down in Luna City, I was making moves on the surface."

Liana struggled against the men holding her down. "I *trusted* you," she snarled. "You used me for information!"

Zale chuckled. "And you were so willing to give it up! Your knowledge of Sea Haven helped me negotiate with this kind man. After you arrived and I heard your story of what had happened to you, I saw an opportunity. I returned to the drillship where I contacted Mister Ray, and he flew out to discuss how we can solve our little *problem* together."

"And what a fine opportunity it was for me," Carson added. "I couldn't have planned for such a turn of events myself. Ocean Rock is in the business of energy resources, and I just so happen to have the means in which to harness and sell one of the most valuable energy resources on Earth."

"So you're expanding on your sick Blue Wave Energy operation," I sneered. "It wasn't enough to steal your own people's magic. Now that you know the Luna pod exists, you'll strip them of their power, too, regardless of whether it's yours to take or not."

"It's power I'm providing him," Zale cut in. "I am a prince of the Luna pod. My father and brother were too weak to do what needed to be done, so it's up to me to decide the fate of the Luna pod."

"How could you?" Tristan demanded.

"I told Father there is nothing left for us in the sea. We've made no progress in two-hundred years, and look at how advanced the humans are! The next logical step is to move ashore, but the pod was intent on ignoring me, so I had to do something to *make* you all listen."

"You're delusional if you think Carson will ever let us go or give your people their magic back," I told him.

"Ha! Delusional?" Zale scoffed. "My father was the delusional one, thinking he can just do nothing and everything will resolve itself."

"If you really feel that way, you could have left," Tristan stated. "You didn't have to take us down with you."

Zale shook his head. "The Luna pod is a sinking ship anyway. Just look at how we harmed that whale to draw you out, and you fell right into our trap! Nothing's changed. You're all still the same idiots who got the queen killed."

I couldn't comprehend the evil that had consumed Prince Zale. He couldn't get people to listen to him, so he thought it better to destroy them completely. He thought being a leader meant making people submit to you, when it was really about listening and moving people into action that benefits the entire group. Worse, Zale was born with access to his full magic, but he was willing to give it up, and everyone else with him, in order to fit into a world that wasn't his own. He couldn't win this by trying to become something he wasn't.

I recalled Zale's speech the night of the fall equinox, and how he spoke of wanting to be more than just a prince. At the time, I thought his desires were much like Tristan's, who believed there were many ways to serve his people beyond the palace. But Zale's ambitions were darker and far more twisted. He believed he could change what it meant to be prince and claim ownership over his people. He thought exerting his power over them made him better than all the monarchs who came before him.

"Don't you use our mother's name in vain," Tristan growled at his brother. "Mother's death was a tragedy, but now you've ensured the rest of us will perish, too."

"*Enough!*" Carson snapped. "You can save your family disagreements for another time. We are here for one thing, and one thing only! Ocean Rock has agreed to partner with Blue Wave Energy *if* we can demonstrate the power we're able to harness. Don't worry—this won't hurt a bit."

I'd heard those words before, and they were as much of a lie now as they were then.

Carson raised the sea stone into the air. All around me, merfolk groaned and hunched over, their shoulders sagging as more power leeched out of them. Agony twisted in my gut, reminding me of the horrible feeling of having my core stolen from me in the basement of City Hall. It was obvious Carson didn't care if he destroyed the Luna pod completely, as long as he got his payday.

The sea stone glowed brighter, until a lightning bolt blasted out of the stone to connect with the clouds above us. The air crackled with static electricity. Carson gave a delighted laugh, while the men surrounding us widened their eyes greedily.

Carson turned toward the men, holding out the glowing stone. "You see how much power they hold? And there's so much more where that came from."

The men holding us back stepped forward, looking intrigued by the power Carson exhibited. They paid us no further attention, as we'd already been rendered completely helpless.

"How much power can you harness at once?" one of Ocean Rock's men asked.

Carson began rambling off numbers, which made the hunger in the men's eyes grow.

Tristan leaned over to me, keeping his voice low. "I'll create a distraction. You go get help."

"Me?" I balked.

"Without our powers, we won't get far, but you still have your fins on. You can swim faster than any of us."

"Carson will notice me gone, and that puts everyone in danger," I hissed.

"If we don't move now, we're already done for," Tristan pressed. "I know you, Bree. You didn't let Carson get away with stealing your magic back in Sea Haven, and we're not letting him take it from us now."

The thought of having fought to restore my core, only to end up at Carson's mercy all over again ignited a rage within me beyond any I'd experienced before. It wasn't just my power at stake this time. It was the magic, lives, and culture of an entire people that would be wiped out if he got what he wanted.

I had mere moments to decide. If I did this, I risked a bullet to the back before I made it off the ship. Otherwise, I could stay here, preserve my life and the lives of the merfolk around me, even if that meant subjecting us all to a bleak and powerless future, stripped of our potential and all that united us.

I realized that was not a life that I wished to keep living. From the moment I entered this battle and swam to Tristan's side, I chose to put my trust in him. I had to believe that this was going to work, too.

And if it didn't, at least my power would *never* end up in Carson Ray's hands ever again.

Tristan shot another glance at the men. "Quickly, while their backs are still turned."

My heart shattered as I considered the possibility that

regardless of whether I slipped away unnoticed, this could very well be the last time I saw Tristan alive. I had to accept the fact that it was something he was willing to risk as well.

"Stay alive," I begged.

Tristan nodded, trembling as he replied, "For as long as I'm able."

My heart hammered as I pressed my heels into the deck and slid backward, the fabric of my skirt slick against the wet deck. While the men were distracted by Carson's presentation, I slunk off into the shadows, my wrists still bound by zip ties. Merfolk ignored me, as to not bring attention to my movements. As I reached the edge of the ship and peered into the deep waters below, I hesitated.

It reminded me of the day I paused to jump off the boat in the lagoon when we first arrived. It became clear to me then why I'd been uncertain to take the leap that day. Things felt safe when all I knew was the limited powers I'd grown up with. The moment I chose to step off that boat and dive into the water, I wouldn't be the same Bree Waters I once knew.

That day, it felt like something I still had the power to choose. Now I knew there were some things you could never come back from. Even without my tail or siren call, I was already forever changed by everything I'd experienced. I couldn't go back to the way things were—only decide what to do moving forward.

I shot a glance behind me, just in time to see Tristan jump to his feet and charge toward the group of men surrounding Carson. He rammed his shoulder into Carson's back, and merfolk erupted into a battle cry as chaos broke out on the ship deck.

This time, I didn't hesitate.

I threw myself off the ship, plunging into the frigid waters below.

CHAPTER 23

I figured I had less than a minute before the chaos aboard that ship settled and Carson noticed me missing. The second that happened, he'd send his powers churning through the sea to sweep me up and return me to his clutches. I didn't think he'd let me live this time.

Which meant I had to get out of the range of his sea stone, to give myself a fighting chance before he could catch me.

I kicked my scuba fins harder than I ever had before to push myself toward the ocean bottom. My pulse roared in my ears, and my breaths came in shallow heaves. I didn't know how far the effect of Carson's sea stone reached, but the closer I got to the bottom, the more it became obvious that even that small piece of sea stone possessed immense power, because my magic was still suppressed.

I reached the sea floor, gulping saltwater as I swung my arms downward onto the edge of a sharp rock. The zip tie binding my wrists snapped, and I regained control of my arms, but I was still helpless against the effects of the sea stone.

My gaze darted around desperately, as if my surroundings could provide me with a plan moving forward. Tristan had helped me escape, but I was on my own now. It was up to me to decide how to save the Luna pod, and I feared we were out of options.

I caught sight of a shadow in the distance that rose from the ocean floor, and I realized where I was. Carson's ship was positioned directly over the shipwreck that Tristan had shown me not long ago.

The shipwreck was in the opposite direction of Luna City, but in a split-second, I'd already made my decision. I kicked my heels off a rock and took off toward the old wreckage. I pumped my arms and kicked my legs, then ducked through the hole in the hull of the ship. I swam over to the treasure chest Tristan had shown me and threw it open.

From outside the cabin, I heard the roar of a massive ocean current rumbling against the rocks. I shot a glance out the window to see a wall of sand and bubbles rushing my way. My heart leapt, because that could only mean one thing. Carson had noticed me missing, and he knew exactly where to find me.

From within the treasure chest, an emerald-cut aquamarine stone caught the light and shimmered a bright blue. I snatched up Queen Lorelei's necklace and threw it around my neck. I quickly secured the clasp, and power flooded back into me as the royal stone counteracted the effects of Carson's weapon.

Drawing my shoulders back, I turned toward the window to face the incoming current head-on. Then, water rose up at my command. My power launched me forward, and I burst out of the window of the shipwreck. I went spiraling though the water and sliced through Carson's oncoming attack like a torpedo. His wave was so powerful that it seemed to close in on me on all sides, the water pressure so strong I couldn't breathe. But the power of my own current rivaled his, and I continued spinning without drawing back.

I gasped a greedy breath as I broke through Carson's wave and out the other side. I clenched my chest to make sure Queen Lorelei's necklace was still there, and I found it secure. The fleeting thought crossed my mind that even though Queen Lorelei was gone, she was somehow still here with us. All our ancestors were, like the way their voices lived on in the island's enchantment.

I knew then exactly what I needed to do.

The current I'd summoned pushed harder to carry me toward Luna City. The faster I moved, the quicker my heart pounded. As I reached the edge of the city, the fabric of my skirt caught against the rushing water, and the waistband slid past my hips to reveal only my shorts underneath. It was only slowing me down, so I yanked on the waistband, and it snapped. The skirt broke free and drifted off into the waters I left behind.

As it did so, it caught on my scuba fins, and those became loose on my feet. I panicked for a moment, until I realized I didn't need them anymore, because the power of the current I'd summoned was enough to carry me wherever I wanted to go.

I kicked the scuba fins off, and they drifted downward into the crevices of the city below. I was left drifting over the city with my legs and feet bare, not hiding or covering up as the mermaid I wished to be, but exposed as the person I was.

Bree Waters.

The girl who never quit.

My heart swelled, causing my power to surge. The current rose up to carry me miles in mere moments. As I passed over Luna City, I glanced down to find it completely abandoned. Noah and the others must've gotten everyone out.

My gaze landed upon the Ancestral Trench, and I spiraled downward to land at its edge. I was gasping for breath by the time my feet hit the sand.

I was struck by how still everything was. Only my footsteps could be heard in the sand as I stepped forward. I clutched Queen Lorelei's aquamarine stone to my chest as I peered into the endless darkness ahead. The pounding of my pulse in my ears quieted, and the roar of the current I'd summoned subsided. I was left standing alone in eerie silence.

"Kraken," I called out. My voice echoed across the vast emptiness. "The Luna pod faces a dangerous foe, and they need your help."

I was only met with silence, and I had to consider the very real possibility that the Kraken had fled, too. That thought terrified me to my very core.

Hopelessness sank in my gut, and I dropped to my knees at the edge of the trench. My gaze fell upon a dull rock in the sand, and I tossed it over the edge, as if one measly little rock was enough of an offering to awaken the Kraken. The rock tumbled into nothingness, and the tentacles I hoped to appear never did.

"Please," I whispered desperately as tears rose to my eyes. "I can't do this alone."

Sobs broke out of my chest as sadness consumed me. I was alone here in Luna City, with no options left to save the people Carson had captured. I had Queen Lorelei's necklace, but all it did was counteract the effects of the sea stone. I'd still have to overpower Carson, and he'd knock me out of the sky before I had a chance to pull a wave over his head. The power of one single mermaid wasn't enough.

A hand landed on my shoulder, and I gave a start. I whirled around, ready to defend myself, but dropped my shoulders when I saw it was Noah. He stared down at me, lips turned into a frown.

"Bree—" he started.

Before he could say anything more, I shot to my feet and threw my arms around his neck. "It's over," I cried. "King Aalto's dead, and Carson Ray is back. He's captured the pod and leeched their powers with the sea stone."

Noah squeezed me closer. "Not everyone's powers."

I drew away, and it occurred to me Noah's blue fins were still swaying in the water. I realized the sea stone's powers must not reach this far.

I peered past him and saw several guards floating at the entrance of a nearby sea cave. This must've been where they moved the citizens to. The guards were suspended there in the water with their scales shimmering in the dim light.

I glanced upward. Carson's ship was a mere shadow upon the surface, but it was coming closer with each passing second. It wouldn't be long until his sea stone came close enough to siphon the rest of the Luna pod's powers, and then he'd have no problem capturing us all.

"If the pod still has their magic this far out from the incoming ship, then we might still be able to use our powers to defeat Carson," I told Noah.

"How are we going to get close enough to fight him?" Noah made a point; as soon as we swam too close to the ship, the sea stone would render our powers useless.

The guards kept their eyes on us, and I realized they were awaiting instruction.

"Bree?" Noah pressed. "How are we going to fight them off?"

"We aren't," I answered. I found the words slipping

from my mouth before I realized they were true. "Noah, we've gone our whole lives beholden to the effects of the sea stone. Maybe it's true we couldn't fight back because we didn't know any better, but what's also true is that we never had the resources to go up against the council, even if we tried. The second we swim within the range of Carson's weapon, we're done for. So we have to do this another way."

"How?" His eyes searched mine for answers, but I didn't have the answers to give him. If we didn't take that ship down by force, I didn't know how else we were going to defeat Carson.

As I was contemplating our options, laughter cut through the air. It wasn't the cold, chilling laughter of a villain like Carson, though. It was the beautiful, joyful laughter of a child. My gaze snapped in the direction of the sound to see a young mergirl swishing her fins to slip past the guards.

"Hey!" the guards called. They lunged for her, but she darted out of their reach.

"Pearl!" her mother cried as she raced out of the sea cave behind her daughter.

It was the little girl I met at the Bar the day Noah and I made sand sculptures and danced to the pod's folk tunes. Her brother and sister, Beck and Maisie, hid in the shadows of the sea cave, peering past the tails of the guards.

Pearl swam up to me and poked at my toes. "I know you!"

"Pearl," her mother, Naia, scolded as she reached us. "We have to return to the sea caves. It's not safe out here!"

"Hang on," I said. "Can I talk to her?"

Naia took Pearl's hand, but she hesitated. "How is a three-year-old going to help?"

"Because she's not scared," I said, before kneeling to Pearl's level. "Do you understand why your family is hiding in the sea caves?"

Pearl nodded. "Mama says there's bad guys on the surface."

"Then why did you come out here?" I asked gently.

Pearl tickled my toes again, appearing fascinated by them. "Because when I met you, Mama said the girl with the legs came here to help us."

My heart melted. It was true that King Aalto had asked for my help when I arrived here, but I wasn't sure there was anything more we could do.

Whispers filled the air, and I lifted my gaze to see hundreds of merfolk slowly emerging from sea cave openings throughout the city. All eyes peered down on me with a curious expression reminiscent of the strange looks I kept getting when I first got here.

There I was, kneeling on the sea bottom with my toes in the sand, looking completely out of place amongst the seafolk. I once didn't feel safe enough to let these people see me for who I was, but I didn't care anymore. This was me—take it or leave it.

Maybe under different circumstances I'd have been able to find my place amongst the Luna pod, but the time for that was over. Still, everyone was staring on expectantly, awaiting answers.

"Bree," Noah said softly. "You defeated Carson Ray once before. Perhaps we can play to his weaknesses."

"No." I rose to my feet, never taking my eyes off the pod surrounding us. "He's already prepared for that. We're not going to win this thing by focusing on weaknesses. We have to utilize our strengths."

"But you said the pod can't fight this," Noah reminded me.

"That's because they aren't fighters," I said. "That first night on the boat in the lagoon, you asked me what I knew about myself, Noah. I told you I always saw the best in people. The best of the Luna pod isn't in their anger and their storms, and they don't need that from me, either. I've watched the Luna pod for weeks, and these people thrive on connection to one another."

"How's that going to help us?" Noah asked.

"Because that's the one thing Carson doesn't have," I pointed out. "You heard Lamar when we got here. The Luna pod hasn't fought a war in two-hundred years. They've been trying to fight Ocean Rock like they can defeat them with war tactics, but all these people know is peace. If we're going to defeat Carson and the men working with him, then we can't force our power. We have to work with what's already there—the same way you can't control the ocean's storms but only bring what's already there to the surface."

Noah furrowed his brow. "And what is that?"

"Their *song*, Noah," I pressed. "King Aalto said the Luna pod's compulsion magic is their greatest weapon, and Tristan said their siren call protects them, but I think they're both wrong. When we came here, I felt protected by the enchantment, but I misinterpreted it. What I was really feeling was connection. These people are always singing and dancing in community common areas, and it's their song that brings them together. It's what's so enchanting about their people. To protect themselves is a byproduct of working together and creating a strong united front. It *starts* with connection, not with protection. To save the pod, we have to create a connection, and the rest will follow."

I looked toward the surface, and Carson's ship was already crossing over Luna City. It would be over top of us in moments, and we were out of time.

The truth was, I knew there was nothing more we could do. We couldn't get all these people out of the sea caves in time to flee, because by the time they got moving, Carson would already be over top of us. He would succeed at siphoning our powers, capture these people, and hold them captive for as long as he could utilize their magic. At this point, it was inevitable.

Noah's features fell, and I knew he understood this truth as well. The only thing we could do was leave the pod with enough hope, so that one day they could come together and break free of Carson's control.

I extended my hand toward Noah. "Sing with me?"

CHAPTER 24

Noah took my outstretched hand. "Let's give them a performance they'll never forget."

All around us, merfolk followed our lead. Pearl curled her fingers around mine, and Naia held on to Pearl's other hand. Maisie and Beck swam out of the sea cave to meet their mother, and the guards followed. Thousands of seafolk emerged from the caves to join hands.

I had to lead them toward hope, though I couldn't lead them in one of their old folk songs I didn't know. There was only one song that I could share with these people.

I opened my mouth, and my voice echoed across the

trench as I started the first verse to the old sea shanty I once sang with Tristan, Liana, and Noah.

Gifted powers of the sea
Our people ruled the waters
The landmen came with their massive ships
And had our people slaughtered

The Luna pod joined in on the second line, their voices overlapping one another in perfect harmony. The ethereal echo of their siren magic reverberated through the sea as we sang together.

Soon we'll witness turning tides
When the land and sea conspire
Once again in harmony
Like the Gods once so desired

We descended into ocean depths
Our home submerged so deep
Lured sailors to their deaths
Anchored our souls to the sea

Soon we'll witness turning tides
When the land and sea conspire
Once again in harmony
Like the Gods once so desired

Overhead, Carson's ship moved closer, until the shadow of his seacraft crept over the Luna pod. Tears pricked my eyes as I witnessed the first of the seafolk's tails split in two, forming into legs. Their song caught in the backs of their throats, and one by one, the voices began to fade, until their beautiful harmonies were replaced by the sound of panicked cries.

It was over. We'd lost.

Beside me, Noah's voice faltered. He choked on his words as his fins disappeared.

"I'm sorry," I whispered. "I'm sorry I couldn't save everyone—"

I was cut off by the sound of a voice booming overhead. Carson used his sonic scream from aboard the ship to carry his voice down to us. "Give it up, Miss Waters. The prince has already given the order, and the Luna pod has surrendered."

My heart crushed at the thought of Tristan up on that boat, bloody and bruised like when Carson had tortured him back in Sea Haven. I thought of Liana trembling helplessly on the deck, and all the other merfolk who'd been captured with no chance of escape. I looked around at the rest of the Luna pod, who were trying desperately to summon their tails but failing. Naia clutched her terrified children close to her.

Noah's gaze dropped to the aquamarine stone around my neck. "Bree, you're the only one left. Keep going."

"I can't," I said with a wavered breath. "This is the end."

Noah took my face in his hands, forcing me to look into his eyes. "No. There's still one verse left. Remember?"

I didn't recall it, not at first. I remembered there was a third verse, but I couldn't think of the words.

Then, Carson called down to us once more. "What will it be, Miss Waters? Will you surrender, or are you intent on fighting until your dying breath?"

Something clicked within me, and the words to the final verse came rushing back. Carson was taunting me, and it was clear he already knew the answer and wished to do the honors of killing me himself. If this was how things ended for me, then I wasn't going out without getting in the final word.

I opened my mouth, and my sonic scream carried my voice through the water, all the way to the surface. As I sang the final verse to the sea shanty, the notes began to change, as if several voices were joining in and overlapping one another—except they weren't. I was singing on my own, and that beautiful harmony was coming from the power of my siren song.

I began to weep. For so long, I had tried to meld my voice with that of the Luna pod, as if I might find my siren call within their old folk tunes or melodies that were new to me. But instead, my siren song was already within me, in this song I'd known for years. I only had to use my voice to connect with others to find it.

Noah let me go, and I began to float higher above the Ancestral Trench and all the Luna pod as my siren song echoed throughout the city.

> *It may take generations*
> *Until this wish of ours takes float*
> *We'll fight until our dying breath*
> *For rising tides lift all boats*

Something miraculous happened then. A rumbling note that wasn't my own rose up from the Ancestral Trench, resonating in harmony with my tune.

At the same time, several large nets were cast off the side of the enemy ship. They were heavy and sank quickly through the water. Merfolk screamed and tried to flee, but without their tails, they barely moved. Carson gave a chilling laugh that shook the seafloor as thousands of merfolk were trapped beneath his netting.

But it was already too late for him. I turned toward the sound of the rumbling note. From within the Ancestral Trench came a brilliant aquamarine light. It shimmered the same blue I'd seen the island light up the night of the enchanting ceremony.

The low note grew louder. Then came a massive tentacle, followed by a second one. I watched in awe as the Kraken emerged, glowing with the enchanting power of the Luna pod's song.

The Kraken was a magnificent creature who towered as high as a skyscraper. He had a big, bulbous head lined with horn-like protrusions above two very large eyes. Eight long tentacles with suction cups the size of cars spanned in all directions. His skin was a speckled orange, and between his tentacles sat a large mouth with lines of razor-sharp teeth.

Overlapping voices like a choir rang out from the Kraken's skin as the enchantment swelled, while he himself sang along. The enchantment was so powerful that even Carson's magical sea stone couldn't combat it. I'd been rendered motionless as I stared up at the incredible creature.

I'd been right about one thing; I just hadn't known it would work. The Luna pod's strength was in the heart of their people, and leaning into their connection had called their heart to the surface.

The Kraken locked eyes with me, and for a moment I feared he might gobble me whole. Instead, he reached out a tentacle and curled it around my waist, lifting me up to the top of his head. My feet sank into his soft, fleshy skin, and I felt secure there as I gripped on tight to one of his horns. The Kraken let out a mournful cry, as if asking how to save everyone.

I pointed to the surface. "The men on that boat threaten our people!" I cried. "We will bring them down before we let them take us!"

A powerful, angry rumble emitted from the Kraken's throat. Then, he kicked his tentacles off the sea bottom, and we began to rapidly ascend.

Carson must've panicked, because a missile fired from the belly of the ship and blasted through the water straight toward us. The Kraken spread his tentacles and opened his mouth. I flinched, but to my amazement, the Kraken consumed the missile. It exploded from within him without so much as disturbing the sea around us. Carson's weapons were no match for a sea creature this large.

We broke the surface of the water, and from my vantage point atop the Kraken's head, I could see *everything*. Every enemy expression morphed into terror as they witnessed the sea beast rising hundreds of feet above them. Several of the men scrambled backward and fell on their asses.

On deck, most of the pod was trapped within large nets and unable to move. Tristan was lying flat on his back, trembling. His face was bloody and bruised. I expected no less from Sea Haven council head Carson Ray, who clutched his precious sea stone tightly.

Zale stood beside him and pointed a gun at Liana's head. He thought his threat would cause me to hesitate, but it merely ignited a rage within me that there was no coming back from.

Everything happened so quickly. I commanded a powerful water jet to blast out of the sea and connect with Zale's hand so hard that the gun was knocked from his grasp. It clattered to the deck several feet away. When Liana saw that she was free, she whirled around and kicked the sea stone out of Carson's grasp. The stone soared high into the air, where the Kraken swiped out one of his tentacles and caught it. The ocean's surface rumbled as he let out an angry cry and crushed the sea stone effortlessly. A loud *snap* reverberated over the open ocean, and then dust rained down from the Kraken's tentacles.

"No!" Carson bellowed.

All at once, magic flooded back into the merfolk. Their legs transformed back into scales, and they thrashed so violently against their restraints that Carson's men backed away.

Tristan used his strength to snap the zip ties binding his wrists. He remained in his human form and pushed himself upright to stand before Carson. "The Luna pod was never yours to take! We will *always* protect what is ours."

Tristan raised his hands, and the rest of the pod followed. I witnessed Cordelia, Maren, and Lamar break free of the nets and join in Tristan's spell with the others. Zale backed away from his own people, trembling.

An impressive maelstrom formed at the seafolk's command, and the ship jerked backward as a swirling vortex gained control of its movements. The Kraken lifted his tentacles, and the terrified men scrambled to jump ship as quickly as possible. Their dying screams turned to gurgles as they were sucked downward by the sea.

Zale turned to flee and launched himself off the side of the ship, before shifting into his tail and darting away.

Carson's eyes widened, and he took several steps back as he stared up at me on the back of the Kraken. "You should not have this kind of power!"

"You're right, I don't," I called down to him. "But the Luna pod does, because they know how to work together.

That's something *you* can never say! You could've been something greater, Carson, but you took people's power for yourself and never learned just how great we all truly were. Now where are all your men?"

Carson's gaze darted around the ship, but he was alone, surrounded only by merfolk who were closing in, thirsting for his blood.

"Spare me!" Carson begged. "I'm a merfolk, too! I'm one of you!"

As if to prove it, Carson shifted, and his legs transformed into a shimmering red tail. He lay there pathetically, smacking his fins against the deck like we could forgive him for what he'd done.

Tristan, who was in his human form, walked straight up to Carson and glared down at him. "The Luna pod lifts each other up, while you tried to crush us. You will *never* be one of us."

Carson's lips curled back. "Let's see how united the Luna pod is without a king!"

Carson lunged for the pistol lying several feet away. He snatched it up and whirled back toward Tristan, but before he could fire off a shot, the Kraken brought his tentacles down on the ship deck. Metal crunched underneath his strength, and the ship snapped in two. Merfolk fell into the water and swam to freedom.

Meanwhile, Carson scrambled for purchase as he went sliding down the tilted deck. He never found a handhold, nor did he reach the ocean. Instead, the Kraken snatched him up, curling the evil man in his tentacles.

Carson let out one last sonic scream that chilled me to the bone, before the Kraken shoved his head into his mouth and bit down. Carson's voice was instantly silenced as the crunch of bone rang out over the ocean. Blood seeped through the water as the Kraken consumed Carson's body, and I relished in the fact that it was truly over this time. Carson Ray could *never* harm another person I cared for again.

The whirlpool sucked up the remaining bits of the broken ship, until every last piece of the enemy and their equipment had been carried far away from Luna City.

Thousands of merfolk broke the surface of the water, until the entire pod was joined together to cheer in victory. It lasted only moments before the pod's applause was abruptly cut off by a rough voice.

"Mark my words—you will all pay for this!" Prince Zale bellowed.

Everyone turned to see Maren and Lamar dragging Zale across the ocean's surface. The prince thrashed his tail, but he couldn't escape the guards' clutches.

"Your Majesty," Lamar addressed Tristan. "What shall we do with him?"

Tristan glared at his brother. "I had high hopes for you, but you not only failed me and Father; you harmed the entire pod. For your acts of treason, I sentence you to a lifetime in prison."

"No!" Zale cried. "You don't get to tell me what to do! I will not go!"

Zale bit down on Maren's arm and smacked his tail

against the back of Lamar's head, which gave him just enough leverage to slip out of their grasp. He flicked his tail and made a run for it, but he didn't make it far before the ocean opened up beneath him and a massive creature leapt out of the water. The mother whale who had been mourning for her daughter caught Prince Zale in her mouth and consumed him whole.

She splashed down against the water's surface, then turned around and swam off as if she had no care in the world.

The Luna pod had gone completely silent in shock, and it took me a moment to process that the mother whale had *eaten* Prince Zale. To be honest, I didn't blame her, and I didn't think the reset of the pod did, either. If anything, she did these people a favor.

Zale had admitted to harming her child, and she had enacted her revenge without hesitation. Prince Zale would not make it out of her stomach alive, and he would spend his last few moments knowing that the very creatures he attempted to sacrifice were the ones who put an end to his cruelty.

"This is not over yet," I called out to the pod on the surface. I pointed toward the drill site. "Ocean Rock continues to threaten the pod by polluting these waters."

Tristan commanded a waterspout to rise up and carry him to my height. His gaze landed upon the queen's necklace I wore. "You've already saved us once. I trust your decisions moving forward."

His tone was soft, and I understood that he wasn't

asking me to be his queen like he did that day at the Choral Sanctuary. But he *was* asking me to stand beside him, to work together to get the job done. I didn't have to be afraid of the invitation anymore, because I knew I didn't have to make the choice alone.

"I trust her, too," someone said.

I looked down from atop the Kraken's head to see Cordelia floating at the surface. That usual spiteful gaze she shared with me had transformed, and she wore an approving smile.

"I told you the day I fitted you for fins that in my pod, we help each other," Cordelia added. "It doesn't matter that you don't have a tail, because you're a mermaid who helped the pod, and so this pod is *ours*."

I never thought Cordelia would show me such kindness, but when she did, something within me shifted. I still had my family and friends back home in Sea Haven, but the Luna pod held my history, and now a piece of my heart. For so long I thought I didn't belong here because my home was back in Sea Haven, but maybe I didn't have to choose between one or the other. Maybe I belonged in both places.

I lifted my head high and called out over the pod. "The island's enchantment only reaches so far, but the Kraken is now enchanted and not bound to one location. We can take our enchantment to them, and as long as he is out there protecting us, these people can *never* return."

"Then let's get rid of them, once and for all," Tristan commanded.

The Kraken gave a cry of agreement, and the rest of the pod joined in. Then, the Kraken sank back into the water, and he used his powerful tentacles to propel us through the water toward the drill site.

The pod followed, and we emerged beneath the base of the drill platform. Screams from men aboard the platform and the drillship filled the air as they witnessed the colossal sea beast emerge.

I let go of the Kraken's horn and dove into the water, joining Liana, Noah, and Tristan on the surface to watch. The Luna pod joined together in song, and the workers began to flee, scrambling onto lifeboats that took off immediately.

As they drifted away, compelled by the siren song to forget what they saw here, the Kraken curled his tentacles around the empty drill platform. He squeezed, and metal groaned and snapped as he dragged the platform and all the drilling equipment on it into the sea.

The sun broke out of the clouds, and warm light shone down on us.

Tristan's shoulders fell in relief. "We've done it. Ocean Rock will never be able to return to this site. They won't even get close, not with the Kraken's enchantment compelling them away."

"What about the drillship?" I asked. "If he tries to destroy it, the pipes will snap and leak pollution into the waters."

"The Luna pod will access the tools aboard the ship

and cap the well," Tristan said. "We don't have to worry about them polluting our waters any longer."

"I want to help," Liana offered.

"Then come," Tristan said, gesturing to Liana to follow.

As she followed behind him, Noah turned to me. "So, you found your siren song. I knew you would. You figured out who you wanted to be, didn't you?"

I thought back to our conversation in the lagoon our first night here. Noah and I had talked about how afraid I was, and how I had to decide if I wanted to remain powerless or become the mermaid I was born to be. But I realized now we'd had it all wrong.

I shook my head. "I didn't have to make that choice, because I already know who I am and want to be. But I thought to become her, I had to go out and find the parts of me that were missing. I thought making a connection with the Luna pod would show me where I belong, like if I could just learn their songs or match the melody I'd unlock something inside me, but the key was within me all along. Only when I decided that I was already enough as I am did my power emerge, because it wasn't about copying what they were doing, but harmonizing with them. I didn't need their song, Noah. I needed to let my own be heard."

Noah glanced down to my legs still treading water. "What about your tail?"

"I'm not sure yet," I mused. "Maybe it will show up one day, and if it never does, perhaps that's okay, too. Having a tail isn't what makes me a mermaid. The seafolk accept me as I am, and they're not going to exile us like Carson did. As long as we're connected to them, we're a part of them and they're a part of us."

"What are you going to do with your siren song now that you have it?" he wondered.

"I'm going to keep singing, because no matter what happens, I know now that our voices can never be drowned out."

CHAPTER 25

The stone I held in my hand scraped against the face of the rock, sending trails of dust to float downward to the ocean floor. I stood on the Landing, humming along to the song the pod sang in the city down below. Noah and Liana were down at the Bar with so many others who'd spent the last few days recovering from the attack. I could hear Sanvi's voice leading the beautiful song in honor of the baby whale who was still healing. According to Sanvi, the pod's sea herbs were working, and the baby whale would survive.

Far off in the distance, in the direction of the drill site, I could hear the Kraken's song resonating a low tune as he joined in. The city was full of hope again, and the townsfolk were coming together later today to discuss plans to restore their ecosystem. Everyone was eager to help, and I had no doubt that in a year from now, the bare Landing I stood upon would be unrecognizable as the pod brought life back to this once thriving reef.

I'd join them in the town square later today, but I needed to do this first.

"What are you doing?" a voice asked from behind me.

I turned to see Tristan swaying his green fins and heading in my direction. "I'm carving. I hope this is okay. It felt like the right thing to do."

I stepped aside to show him the carving I'd made upon the rock face.

He swam closer to run his fingers over the ridges, reading the words aloud. *"We are Sea Haven."*

"I fell in love with this place when I got here, and I was afraid I'd have to choose between Luna City or my home," I explained. "But now I feel like I can belong to both. I don't have to leave my home behind to find a place here, do I?"

Tristan shook his head. "No, Bree, you don't. I've been trying to tell you all along this place is a part of your history. And now Sea Haven gets to be a part of ours. That's why I came to find you."

I furrowed my brow. "Is everything all right?"

"Everything's great in Luna City, but we promised each other we weren't just going to save my pod," he said. "Carson wasn't the only person on the council stealing Sea

Haven's power. You heard him—that sea stone he had was just one of many. There are still council members back onshore who are stealing Sea Haven's merfolk powers. We should talk about what to do moving forward before the town meeting."

I glanced to the city below, where voices swelled upward to reach the Landing. "Let's go somewhere quieter."

Tristan and I swam toward the surface. We emerged near Crystal Cove, and he transformed into his legs to climb onto the rock beside me. I sat near the waterfall, lifting my chin toward the warm sun as it dried me off.

"If I'm being honest, Tristan, I didn't know how much I was asking of you when we came here," I admitted. "The fact is, we can't take everyone with us. Most of these people aren't equipped to handle this kind of fight, let alone do it with the power of a sea stone affecting them. These people have families here, and they need to focus on restoring your coral reefs and cultivating the fish populations. I want to go back to Sea Haven and show my people just how much they're capable of, but I don't know how many men the Luna pod is able to spare."

Tristan opened his arms wide. "I'm king. There are more than enough people who are willing to follow me."

I smiled. "Then I guess we have ourselves the army we came here for. Thank you, Tristan. For everything. I don't think I'd have found my siren call without you. I have this power because I believed in it so hard that I was willing to die for it. You showed me so much beauty and magic here, and it gave me something worth fighting for."

"There's no need to thank me," he said. "That fighting spirit has been in you all along."

"And your power to lead was always within you," I told him.

I reached up to unclasp Queen Lorelai's necklace. I'd been waiting for Tristan to ask for it back, but I couldn't keep waiting for him to initiate the conversation. I was just as much in the wrong for holding out. If I wanted clear communication, I needed to be forthcoming about my own feelings.

"Here," I said, holding it out to him. "I know you want me to have this, but it belongs to you. You say you need a partner to help you make decisions, but you already have the pod, Tristan. You don't need someone else to tell you what to do, because you already know what's best for them."

Tristan took the necklace. "I understand if you don't wish to be queen. When I told you how I felt about you, I didn't realize just how much pressure that came with. I care deeply about you, Bree, but if you don't wish to be with me, or to hold the responsibility of what that would mean, then I will not ask anything more from you."

"That's not what this is about, Tristan," I said.

The truth was, I cared deeply for him, too. I hadn't forgotten how his kiss made my heart soar, but I couldn't deny that I still had feelings for Noah, too. To make a decision on either of them moving forward, I had to be sure of what my heart wanted, and I wasn't in the place to make that kind of choice right now.

"Maybe one day I could see myself being a queen at your side," I told him. "But I couldn't fulfill that role until I knew that you wouldn't fall apart without me there. I don't want you to become the kind of king your father was after your mother died. Whether there's a future between us or you choose another partner, I think you need the time to learn what kind of a king you are on your own."

Tristan curled his fingers around his mother's necklace. "That right there, Bree, is why I wish to have you by my side. I admire your ability to see the good in people but allow them to come to their greatness at their own pace."

"You have that trait within you, too," I pointed out. "In fact, I think it was you who taught me that. You never pushed me too hard in our training. You only kept trying different things to see which would work for me. And Tristan..."

I placed my hand over his. "I'm not going anywhere. I don't have to be queen to be at your side until this is all over."

Tristan smiled. "If you will not be beside me as queen, then I am more than happy to have you beside me as a friend."

Something clinked against the rocks below us, capturing both of our attention. I looked down to see a glass bottle floating on the surface of the water, the ripples from the waterfall pushing it to the edge of the cove.

"What's that?" Tristan mused. He climbed down the

rocks to pull the bottle from the water. "There's something in here."

As he sat back down beside me, I realized the bottle was corked at the top and there was a piece of paper inside.

I cocked an eyebrow. "A message in a bottle? That's... odd."

Tristan pulled off the cork. "I don't find it strange at all. Remember I told you merfolk used to enchant bottles like this to send messages between pods? Perhaps one of these old messages survived."

He tipped the bottle upside down and emptied the paper into his hand. It was stark white and rolled into a scroll.

"That doesn't look old to me..." I started to say, but as he unraveled it, my heart stopped. My gaze roamed over the words, scrawled upon the paper in sharp letters. I recognized the handwriting.

> *The council has sealed off the town. Cores are being stripped from all who know the truth. We cannot wait for assistance any longer. We must act now, before all is lost.*

"This came from Sea Haven," Tristan realized breathlessly. "How can we be sure someone isn't trying to mislead us?"

I swallowed the lump in my throat, and my voice came out sounding hollow. "Because this came from my father, and this message was meant for me."

We'd saved the Luna pod when we took Carson down, but I hadn't anticipated how his absence would radicalize the rest of the Sea Haven Council. They'd moved on from siphoning magic to downright stripping people of their source of power entirely.

For the first time, the path ahead was clear to me.

Sea Haven was in more danger than ever... and it was up to us to stop it.

END OF BOOK TWO

Return to Sea Haven in book three, *Crashing Waves*.

ABOUT THE AUTHOR

Alicia Rades is a USA Today bestselling author of young adult and new adult paranormal fiction. When she's not dreaming up magical stories, she's either binge-watching paranormal TV shows, meditating, or spending time with her family. She has an unhealthy obsession with psychic characters and writes with a deck of tarot cards next to her computer.

www.ingramcontent.com/pod-product-compliance
Lightning Source LLC
LaVergne TN
LVHW040045080526
838202LV00045B/3489